Beth Goobie

The Dream Where the Losers Go

ORCA BOOK PUBLISHERS

Library and Archives Canada Cataloguing in Publication

Goobie, Beth, 1959-
The dream where the losers go / Beth Goobie.
Originally published: Montreal: Roussan, 1999.

ISBN 1-55143-455-5

I. Title.

PS8563.O8326D74 2006   jC813'.54   C2005-907728-X

Summary: Trying to escape the horror that forced her to attempt suicide,
Skey dreams of a dark tunnel, a place where she is safe and alone.

First published in the United States 2006
Library of Congress Control Number: 2005938899

Orca Book Publishers gratefully acknowledges the support for its publishing
programs provided by the following agencies: the Government of Canada
through the Book Publishing Industry Development Program (BPIDP), the
Canada Council for the Arts, and the British Columbia Arts Council.

The author gratefully acknowledges the Canada Council
grant that funded the writing of this book.

Cover design and photography: Danielle Hogan

Orca Book Publishers   Orca Book Publishers
Box 5626, Stn.B,   PO Box 468
Victoria, BC Canada   Custer, WA USA
V8R 6S4   98240-0468

Printed and bound in Canada
Printed on 50% post-consumer recycled paper, ancient forest friendly,
processed chlorine free using vegetable, low VOC inks.

09 08 07 06 • 5 4 3 2 1

for scott

CHAPTER ONE

SHE BEGAN DREAMING about him in the dark dream, the one with the endless tunnels, stone walls that slid by cold under her fingertips, invisible because it was too dark to see. In this dream, there was no light. Everything came to her by touch or feeling—sadness a heavy salt in her mouth, fear ringing loud bells in her ears. In this dream she was always alone, in air that smelled of damp stone and mildew, her bare feet wet from small puddles, trickles of water that ran down the walls. Hand outstretched, she would touch her fingers to the wall and begin to move forward, never knowing if she was progressing toward an exit that would get her out of this place or if at some point she had turned around and begun moving back toward the place she had come from, a place she could not remember. Dreaming this dream, she had two choices—to move or not to move. She could stay forever lost in one place in the dark or feel herself forward by fingertip along the cold stone walls, moving toward some kind of meaning, some possible place of hope.

Sometimes a draft blew across her and she would think she was approaching a door or gate, perhaps a crack in the wall through which she could look out onto another world and call for help. Every now and then she would hear the shifting or rattling of stones and stop, shock ricocheting through her, but the stones always silenced themselves. Nothing more came with them, no footsteps, no voice.

Until the night she heard him for the first time. She had been feeling her way along a tunnel, stopping at intervals to trace the etchings and hieroglyphs carved into the rock. Messages from another time, another mind. Had they been carved by candlelight or in the dark, the artist deciding by fingertip where to place the next line or curve? Sometimes she could tell she was feeling out a human figure, sometimes it seemed to be a bird, sun or moon. This particular tunnel had been rich with carved figures, stories under her fingers she seemed close to understanding, meaning just beyond her grasp. Then, abruptly, she arrived at a meeting place, a small open area where several tunnels met. She had come across this setup before and had learned to feel her way around the central area, counting the tunnel mouths. There could be any number—as few as four or six. Around one huge cavern, she had counted twenty-one, in another, thirteen. It never seemed to matter which tunnel she chose to enter. Her journey continued always the same, the slow stumbling onward, led by the feel of rough stone and the unseen carvings that slipped by under her fingertips.

When the wall under her right hand disappeared, she edged to the left, checking to see whether the tunnel was ending or widening, then began moving slowly around the outside of the open area to count the tunnel mouths. For the moment, she avoided the center of the meeting place. A few of these places had opened onto large pits, and she had learned to listen ahead of herself for a growing echo on her footsteps, a deepening of sound. There had been none this time, but still she knelt, searching for a rock to roll forward into the center so she could listen for the drop.

From the other side of the meeting place, she heard him. The sound of his breathing seemed to rise out of her own, as if they breathed in parallel rhythm, his slightly heavier, harsher. There was a small grunt, then the sound of a rock rolling across the floor until it came to a gentle stop against her foot. Still on one knee, she froze as if caught in sudden headlights, as if she could be seen by anyone come hunting through these tunnels. Someone who could see in the dark. She waited, listening to the sound of the other, his breathing, the shuffling of his feet as he felt his way around the outside of the meeting place, slipped into a tunnel mouth and continued on.

Still on her knees, she listened to his sounds fade. When fear stopped slamming through her, she closed her hand over the rock that had rolled against her foot. Small with rough edges, it was slightly wet, as everything in this place. She stood, warming it in her palm, then continued around the outside of the meeting place. Five tunnel mouths passed until she thought she had found the one he had taken. There was no sound of him now, but she moved into the sixth tunnel, feeling her way along with her left hand, the rock gripped in her right, following him further into the dark.

SKEY WOKE HOLDING the rock in her hand. At first she didn't notice it. She had been jolted out of sleep by the muffled sound of Ann's radio in the next room. "Win a free trip to Disneyland," blared through the thin wall. Ads about success, fame and fortune. Lying in her narrow bed, Skey watched the elm tree outside her window, its stripped branches riding the wind. Gradually the dark tunnels and the endless feel of stone slipping under her fingers faded, and she rose out of the dark of her dream into the uncertain light of an early November Saturday morning.

Loud laughter came from the unit's kitchen. Some of the girls were making breakfast. Through her closed door, Skey could smell toast and eggs. A flicker of thought crossed her face and she frowned slightly. Five months in this place and Monday, finally, they were going to let her return to her old school. She could come and go into the world beyond her bedroom window again. Dully, Skey stared at the elm branches lifting and falling. More thoughts flickered across her face. An in-between place—that was what it was, lying in her bed like this, watching the elm before she got up. It always told her something about her life. The way it had been. The way it was going to be. *Keep going, keep going*, it seemed to say. Skey lay in her bed and watched until the very lift and fall of those black branches moved into her and she began breathing their rhythm.

Keep going.

Someone knocked on her door and a male voice called, "Skey?"

"Yeah yeah," she mumbled. It was staff, telling her to rise and shine. "I'm *up*," she stressed.

"All *right*," said the voice.

As the staff moved on to Ann's door, Skey began to inch her body toward a sitting position. Bad as her dreams got, the day wasn't anything she wanted to move into. So she usually started it by playing with the concept of getting up, practicing for the actual act. Did this foot belong to this leg? Did this bum belong underneath this back? Did this head belong on this neck or had the wind blown it on by mistake? Was this really someone else's hand stuck on her arm and was it reaching for her throat, about to strangle her?

Skey noticed she was holding something. Drowsily she focused on her right hand and saw the rock. She remembered. She had been dreaming the dark dream, and there had been someone else there. He had rolled this rock across the floor of a meeting place to check for a pit, and she had picked it up. She must have come out of the dream still holding it in her hand.

Jerking upright, Skey stared at the rock. This was *impossible*. Motionless, she sat and stared at the impossible rock until staff knocked at her door again. Somehow she managed a second, "Yeah yeah." Then, when she heard the staff walk away, she got out of bed and took the one full step that covered the width of her small room. Here she set the rock carefully on her dresser. Gray with white markings, it had a few rough edges—a very average looking rock. Pushing it with her finger, Skey listened to the slight scraping sound. Gradually, her bright fear subsided. It might be an impossible rock, but it wasn't dangerous. It wasn't going for her throat, at any rate.

As she dressed, she watched the rock sit on her dresser. Remnants of the dream still clung to it; she thought she could see several hazy tunnels stretching out from it in various directions. Perhaps her room had become a meeting place, the rock its center.

"Rock, you are the last thing I need," Skey muttered. "Day and night mixed together. Day's bad enough on its own. Night's worse."

Opening her socks-and-underwear drawer, she buried the rock under a pile of cotton and polyester. The dark hazy tunnels wavered and almost wisped out. Not quite.

It's an improvement, Skey thought grimly and opened her door onto yet another day on the inside.

THAT NIGHT SHE heard nothing of the other traveler and woke Sunday morning having spent another night alone, feeling her way through the dark. Lying in bed, her eyes closed, Skey could still feel the tunnel wall pressed against her palm. At the same time, she could hear some of the girls making breakfast and the unit's stereo blasting. As she lay motionless, the dream began to fade, but not completely. It never faded completely. During the day, she could tune in and out of it. It was a matter of changing focus—tune out the real world, tune in the dream. She could be anywhere, playing pool with staff or at the school run for the girls in this lockup. She could be here in this room, staring through her bedroom window which had been strengthened by criss-crossing wires so a girl couldn't break her way out. All she had to do was focus inside, and the real world would disappear and the dark tunnel move in to surround her, solid and dense, slowed like a dream.

Skey liked to play with this. In daylight the dream seemed safer, more like a game. She would sit in the middle of a class, tune everything out and find herself standing in a tunnel, tracing a design carved in the rock wall. While she was doing this, she could still see the classroom, but it would look hazy and indistinct, as if *it* was a dream and the dark tunnel was real. Sometimes, as she sat in a classroom, tracing an outline in a tunnel wall, she couldn't decide what the carving looked like, but a meaning would creep into her skin.

This is a human heart, she would think. *This is a sigh. This picture is crying.*

SUNDAY EVENING, Terry called her into the office. The small, brightly lit room looked out onto the unit's open area, its large window strengthened by wire so no girl could break her way in. When a girl was called into the office, the rest of the girls would gather in the unit and watch her talk to staff, read her lips. Skey sat in the chair farthest from the window, avoiding Terry's eyes. Terry was tough, in her forties. Her body had the shape of a woman, but she carried it like a man, holding her shoulders straight and wide, swaggering her hips and scuffing her feet. When she spoke, her voice was jovial and loud, full of tease, but her dark eyes watched carefully, always assessing. Warm, Terry was warm. When someone said something to her, she took it in. She listened to a girl the way she listened to another staff.

"So, you ready for your first day back at school? Your own school?" Leaning back in her chair, Terry grinned and watched.

Skey sat curved in a chair opposite, shoulders so tense they hurt. "I guess," she mumbled.

"It'd make me kind of nervous going back to my old school after I'd been gone a few months," Terry said easily.

"Yeah, I guess." Skey fixed her eyes vaguely on the office's locked medicine cabinet. It was one thing having a laugh with staff while playing a game of pool, but that didn't mean she wanted to be hauled into the office so she could spill her guts on command.

"So, you feel all right about it?" Terry probed. "You know where your homeroom is?"

"I've been going to that school for two years now." Skey shrugged.

"And you're comfortable with the visit we made to your school principal?" Terry asked. "The guidelines he laid out for you?"

"I guess," Skey said.

Terry paused, searching for a way to open her up—the correct combination of words, the right tone of voice. There might be one. Skey held herself stiff and waited.

"Did you know," Terry said slowly, "that there are five people employed full-time just to scrape gum off the Statue of Liberty?"

"Huh?" Startled, Skey glanced at Terry's grinning face.

"Yeah," said Terry. "I read that somewhere. So if you ever need a job scraping gum off a wall, just fly to New York and apply to work at the Stature of Liberty. Forty hours a week. Probably minimum wage."

"Maybe when you let me out of this place," Skey said with a slight grin. "Give me a reference?"

"You bet." Without losing a beat, Terry twisted the subject back to school. "You sure you're okay with everything?"

Skey closed down, dropping her eyes. "I guess."

"Skey?" If Terry was waiting for a response, she wasn't going to get one, but her voice ambled on cheerfully. "What's your favorite color?"

Skey sat, thinking her way through the options. She knew it wasn't black—she got more than enough of the dark in her dreams—but it wasn't white either. White didn't help you see things any better. "It depends," she said slowly.

"On what?" asked Terry.

"On my mood." Skey spoke hesitantly, thinking out loud into Terry's listening silence. "I guess it's this color you can find sometimes between a peach and a pink. Not exactly peach and not exactly pink. Some days I like green, other days it's blue."

"Like the sky?" asked Terry.

"Like the sky around three o'clock in the afternoon when it's really hot," said Skey.

Terry gave her a slow smile. "Now you're talking."

"It's really hot," said Skey, "and the radio's playing. And you're lying in the sun, and you've got nothing to do, and you could do anything you wanted. That's the color of sky I like best." She paused, still thinking. "But most days I like gray. Gray because it's quiet."

Terry nodded. "Skey, help me with something. When I'm working the morning shift and you're leaving for school, tell me what color you're feeling."

Briefly, Skey's eyes flickered across Terry's. "Why?"

Terry shrugged. "When I wonder how you're doing at school, I'll think of that color."

Skey moved in and out of Terry's gaze, leaving it, coming back, leaving it again. Coming back. "That's weird, Terry," she said finally.

"Hey, I thought of it myself," said Terry.

THAT NIGHT SKEY stood at her window, holding the rock. There was no wind. The elm's branches reached out sharp and clear, motionless against the stars. As motionless as the large black iron gate that stood at the far end of the lock-up's parking lot, dividing the grounds from the street. The gate's purpose seemed to be decoration—it stood open day and night, cars and people coming and going. Skey's eyes skimmed the staff-and-visitor parking lot, then settled on the concrete building that housed the school gym and classrooms beyond it. She had lost the previous September and October in that building. Autumn had been a daze of green leaves turning amber in the windows, the buzz of flies growing slower against window glass until they

died. Floor hockey games, roller-skating, arts and crafts—
she had done what she had been told to do, fulfilled their
expectations for good behavior. Tomorrow morning they
would have to open one of their precious doors and let her
out.

The moon was somewhere in the middle of itself, half
dark, half light, the ground shadowy with dead grass and
leaves. No snow yet. How she longed to walk out into those
stars and feel the breeze move over her skin, feel herself move
inside like something in the dark you can't see but know is
there, going on about its business. Unseen but always going
on, like a heart.

The rock seemed to pulse in her hand. Skey half
expected it to glow with a strange light, but it had come out
of the dark. It was impossible and a mystery, but it held no
messages—just a gray rock with rough edges that had acci-
dentally bumped against her foot. A dream rock.

A dreaming rock, Skey mused, turning it over. Maybe she
was the rock's dream, and the rock was hers. She laughed
softly.

"You've been here too long, loser," she whispered. "Soon
you'll belong."

Leaving the window, she crawled into bed and turned
to face the wall. Sometimes she and Ann tapped back and
forth, but tonight she could hear the other girl's snores.
Gently Skey tightened her grip on the rock, and suddenly
she was in the dream tunnel, standing somewhere in the
dark. Stretching out her left hand, she located the wall and
began to feel her way along. Almost immediately, she heard
him—the other one. Everything in her stopped. Abruptly,
from nearby, came the sound of a heavy stone shifting,
followed by a muffled curse.

She crept forward, so alert her joints felt about to snap. Whoever the other one was, he seemed to be seated, nursing his foot and muttering to himself. It wasn't an intelligent monologue, nothing like Hamlet—just a long string of swear words, slowly and meticulously phrased, as if pronouncing them with the utmost care was keeping everything in place, containing the hurt until it subsided. From the sound of his voice, he seemed to be fifteen or sixteen, around her own age. Quietly she stood, trying to silence her breathing as she listened to the boy feel his way through pain. After a while he stood and began to move forward, swearing every now and then, and she followed at a short distance, holding the small rock in her hand.

CHAPTER TWO

THERE WAS A KNOCK on her door. "Skey," said a female voice. "It's time to get up."

"Yeah yeah," mumbled Skey.

"C'mon," said the voice. "It's your first day back at school."

"Yeah yeah," said Skey. "I heard you."

The rock lay in her hand, warm as flesh. Sitting up, Skey stared at it. All night she had followed the boy through the darkness of her dreams. This rock kept him close, she was certain of it. The night she had left the rock in her dresser drawer, she hadn't heard him, but last night she had encountered him as soon as she entered the dark tunnel. It was this rock that connected them, it had to be.

Should she take it to school with her or leave it here? What if staff sprang a room search on her while she was gone and went through her stuff? Would they take it? But if she took the rock to school with her, would she lose it? Finally, Skey decided to keep the rock in a front pocket of her jeans, checking first for holes. Then she positioned herself in front of her mirror and applied her makeup. Not the heavy metal, headbanger face most of the girls here wore—Skey sketched herself in thin delicate lines, a face for the cover of *Seventeen*.

OPENING HER BEDROOM door, Skey entered the unit's common area. To her left were four bedrooms, the unit TV and stereo and the washroom; to her right, the office and kitchen area. Directly opposite were five more bedrooms. Quickly, she passed the couches and pool table that sat in the middle of the unit, picked up some toast and juice sitting on a kitchen counter and joined two girls, Ann and Monica, at one of four small tables. Several girls sat haphazardly at the other tables—a lunch-and-supper seating plan was posted by the fridge, but at breakfast a girl could sit where she wished. Quietly envious of Skey's impending freedom, Ann and Monica didn't say much. Most of their attention was focused on Viv, a new girl who was still in her room, yelling at staff. Admitted three weeks ago, Viv was still going through the adjustment stage, throwing her weight around and emphasizing herself with threats and volume. Today she seemed to be refusing to get up.

"You gonna run?" Ann mumbled through a mouthful of toast. As usual, her eyes were shifting nervously, her body jerking every time Viv banged or yelled. Carefully Skey slid her eyes across Ann's face. Ann was thin, thinner than Skey, and she didn't have to work at it. But her long black hair was ratty. She needed to wash it.

"No," Skey said shortly. She hadn't considered going AWOL. She wanted to leave this place for good, not get dragged back by cops.

"I dunno if I could go back to my old school," said Monica.

"Not if everyone knew I lived here. Why didn't you ask for a new school?"

Monica had gained seven or eight pounds since her admission last summer, and she kept eating. As the pale blond girl started her second bowl of cereal, Skey pushed aside her own half-eaten toast, plain with no butter. Standing up, she said, "I have to brush my teeth."

"Hey, Skey." Ann twisted a strand of her long limp hair, her sharp wrist bones shifting under her skin like a dance. Fascinated, Skey stared. All of Ann's bones were like that, rippling the surface. *Beautiful.*

Catching her gaze, Ann grinned, her teeth startlingly white against her dark skin. "If you get some stuff," she said, "share it, eh?"

"Yeah yeah," said Skey.

She brushed her teeth, then followed staff down the three flights of stairs that led to the lockup's side entrance. As the woman's key slid into the lock, Skey's entire body tensed. What if the key got stuck; what if the lock didn't turn; what if she was trapped in here forever? With a groan, the door swung open, and she could smell the November wind, the leaves and the cold, cold air. From inside the door, it looked like another world out there, the life of a different person blowing by.

Smiling slightly, staff handed her two bus tickets. "You'll be back by 4:30?" she asked.

"Yeah yeah," said Skey.

"Got your lunch?" the woman asked. "Have a good day."

"Do I have to?" asked Skey. "Or can I take a break?"

THEY WERE IGNORING her or waiting for her, it was hard to tell which. Through the bus window, Skey watched Rosie and Balfour smoking in the student parking lot. Her heart splattered, rain hitting glass. How she wanted to get off the bus, raise her head with a knowing smile, let the wind lift out her long dark hair and saunter over to them as if she had never been gone and was still part of them—part of their invisible force field that ran Wellright High, ran it with smirks and sneers, whatever the occasion demanded.

But she couldn't. Face pressed to the glass, Skey couldn't find the vibe, the attitude, the correct brain wave that would place her back in May of last year, before everything changed, and she was pulled out of the real world into the inside of her head, where nothing fit together and very little made sense. Staring out the window, she swallowed and swallowed. Birds kept flying up her throat, birds of heat and salt. Their cries filled her head. Dropping her eyes, she rode the bus for another block, then got off and entered the school by the tech wing's door, an entrance that couldn't be seen from the student parking lot.

Incredibly it had all remained the same. To the right and left, rows of lockers opened and slammed, kids shoved stuff in and pulled things out. Fluorescent lighting flickered overhead, and here and there Skey could see erratic gaps where guys had taken running leaps and poked out a ceiling tile. In the middle of the surrounding mayhem, she stood with one hand to a wall, tracing the shape of a concrete block. So, the school was still here, and so was she. That much came together. For now.

She started toward the locker the principal had assigned her, thinning herself down, weaving in and out of the flow of bodies and voices. Coming into the school, she had pulled up her jacket hood and now she kept it up. No one recognized her, no one called out. Last year these had been kids she knew; she had dropped into their jokes and laughter as if she owned it, as if it would always be hers. Now it was like walking through a magazine that had suddenly come to life in all the expected images, but they were too vivid, startling her with color and sound.

Taking a deep breath, she turned into the hall that led to her locker then froze in fear as she saw Gillian and Pedro leaning against the wall directly opposite her locker. No question about it this time. They were definitely waiting for her.

Gillian's mother was one of the office secretaries. Either Gillian had wheedled the locker number out of her, or she'd somehow gotten into the school's database. It wouldn't have been that difficult; she had accessed information for the Dragons before. That was why they had decided to include Gillian as a fringe member—she was adept at leaving casual fingerprints all over the school office.

Skey began a casual drift backward. She had thought she would be able to handle this, find the same old face and drag out the same old laugh. But that face and laugh belonged to the self she had lost last spring, a self she could no longer reach. Somehow she had made herself believe that part of her, that lost self, had been left behind here at Wellright High, wandering these halls like a ghost and waiting for her body to show up so they could connect and she would be whole again, the same old Skey Mitchell.

But the lost self wasn't here. Skey couldn't feel her anywhere. That meant she was stuck being the pale, quiet, nothing-to-say, not-worth-noticing, very fucked-up, locked-up head case, except now she would be displaying it to her friends. No, former friends. They wouldn't give her five minutes like this. Jigger wouldn't. No one would.

Skey turned and headed for homeroom. The halls were thinning out now, students rushing to beat the warning bell, but still she kept her hood up and her head down. Coming down a stairwell, she scanned ahead for anyone who might be waiting in the hall outside her homeroom, then realized too late that she had forgotten a small open area behind the stairs. As she stepped off the bottom stair, sudden hands reached out and pulled her in. Frantically, Skey fought the scream that surged through her. It was always like this now—someone touched or spoke unexpectedly and the scream started, low in her gut. She had to fight so hard to keep it quiet.

"Skey, how ya doin?!" At least a foot taller than Skey, Trevor grinned down at her. He placed a large football hand on her shoulder, and she saw he was still wearing the Rolex watch he had "borrowed" from an uncle's dresser drawer last Christmas. His favorite joke was that he wore it all the time and his parents never noticed. Behind him, San fluttered her fingers in a wave. A triangle of gold sequins glimmered at the corner of her mouth.

"Hey, I'm here, aren't I?" Backing against the wall, Skey tried out a laugh. Trevor followed, closing in.

"What they give you to eat in that place?" Taking her lunch bag, he opened it. "Bread and water?" he said incredulously. "Got any Ritalin?"

He was so close, Skey could feel his breath on her face. She could also feel the shakes coming. "I'm not on anything," she said quickly.

"Tuna fish!" Sniffing one of her sandwiches, Trevor made a face. "No one's gonna want you if you smell like this," he drawled.

"Not even Jigger," added San, pushing past him and

draping herself over Skey's shoulder. A heavy cloud of Eternity settled around them both.

"Lay off, San," Skey hissed.

Trevor and San exchanged knowing grins. "Jigger's still interested," cooed San. "You haven't turned into a nun, have you?"

"Give me some air, would you?" Panicking, Skey gave the other girl a slight shove.

"Don't get pushy," Trevor said immediately.

"I just want to breathe," Skey mumbled.

She could feel their eyes on her, watching for changes. Dragons' eyes. Skey had seen them watch other kids like this, kids on the outside, prey.

"Hey, what's with you guys?" she asked, smiling weakly.

"We just wanted to welcome you back," Trevor said. The warning bell rang, cutting him off, and he waited for it to finish. "Wanted to let you know everything's still the same with us," he continued easily.

And you, Skey, are you the same? The question wavered, unspoken, but Skey felt it as if it had been carved into the air between them and she was tracing its meaning with her finger. Then came the answer, also unspoken and carved into the air.

I didn't tell. I didn't tell any of the Dragons' secrets.

Trevor's lips parted in a wide grin. "Enjoy your tuna fish sandwich," he said.

San fluttered another wave. "See you at lunch."

They left, tearing up the stairwell. As Skey watched them go, the hallway began to fade out around her and the dream tunnel moved in. Relieved, she welcomed the darkness. Finally she could be alone, without name, without face, without expectations. Maybe she would find the message here, the meaning that would explain everything. It would tell her what to do, who she needed to become.

But as she reached out to touch the tunnel wall, she realized she could still see the school hallway. The real world hadn't completely faded and the two realities overlapped. Several kids walked by, glancing at her. One stopped to stare. With a hiss, Skey pulled out of the dark tunnel and bent to retrieve her lunch from where Trevor had dropped it. Then she gave a cold glare to the kid who stood close by, watching her. A short kid—first year twerp.

"You all right?" he asked.

Skey threw all her focus into staring him down. Reddening, he shrugged and turned away. Alone beside the staircase, Skey paced her breathing until she could no longer hear it coming back at her off the walls. Then she lowered her jacket hood and walked grimly toward what was expected of her.

Homeroom was already in session. She had missed the national anthem and morning announcements. Kids sat talking at their desks, and the homeroom teacher, Mr. Pettifer, was looking over some notes. Hesitantly, Skey stepped through the open doorway and waited. Sensing her presence, Mr. Pettifer looked up. "Skey," he said with a smile. "Come in. We have a seat for you in the front row."

The front row. Everyone's eyes would be on her back. Swiftly, Skey scanned the room and saw several empty seats, the closest by the wall, three desks from the back. She walked over to it.

"How about here?" she asked.

Mr. Pettifer nodded. "Fine."

A sigh heaved through Skey. Now, finally, everyone's eyes would let her go. They would stop watching. Quickly, she

slid into the seat, angling her body so the desk caught her
butt as her knees buckled. Seated, she was breathing openmouthed as if there wasn't enough air, staring at the place
where the classroom's front wall met the ceiling—a thin line
of darkness where two planes met, intersected and opened
into another dimension. This time Skey let go completely.
Instantly the classroom disappeared and the dark tunnel
surrounded her. But she kept her head, didn't stretch out a
hand to feel her way along the wall—not with a classroom
of kids watching her in the real world. Instead, she slipped
her hand into her pocket and closed it around the rock.

Immediately she heard the boy, so close she could have
reached out and touched him. It was his breathing she heard
first, short and rasping. Not as if he had been running—it
was fear she heard scraping at his throat. He was muttering,
"Someone's here, I can feel it. Someone's close." A long series
of swear words followed. "Someone's after me," the boy whispered. "Someone's going to find me." Then there was only
silence, the two of them waiting each other out in the dark,
Skey holding the rock to keep them close and breathing as
quietly as possible so he wouldn't bolt and leave her alone.

She came out of it to find Mr. Pettifer's face leaning in
on hers. "Skey," he said, observing her carefully. "I've set
up an appointment for you today with Ms. Renfrew in the
Counseling office. It's at 12:30, so you won't have to miss
any classes."

Alarm shot through Skey and she asked, "Why do I have
to go to the Counseling office?" Staff were already coming
out of her ears. The last thing she needed was more therapy.

"We've got to figure out what you've missed so you can
catch up," Mr. Pettifer said mildly. "Ms. Renfrew will contact
your teachers to see where you need the extra help."

"Oh," mumbled Skey. Well, it would be a way to avoid her lunch-hour session with San and the rest of the gang. And Jigger—*if* he really wanted to talk to her.

"Are you feeling well?" Mr. Pettifer was still scrutinizing her closely. "You look pale."

"I'm fine." Glancing down, Skey noticed she had pulled the rock out of her pocket and was cradling it on her open palm. Fear flashed through her. Had Mr. Pettifer seen the rock? Would he think it was a weapon, like lockup staff would, and take it away?

"It's just a rock, nothing important," she muttered, closing her hand over it and clenching tightly.

"What rock?" asked Mr. Pettifer.

He hadn't seen the rock. Had he simply not noticed it, or was the rock not real? If it wasn't real, then she, Skey Mitchell, was completely, certifiably crazy.

But maybe it made sense that Mr. Pettifer couldn't see the rock. After all, it had come out of her own private dream. It belonged to her mind, her heart. Why would it be a surprise that something that meant everything to her couldn't be seen by other people?

"Sorry," said Skey, shoving the rock back into her pocket. "My mind wanders, you know. Sometimes it gets lost, and I have to go looking for it."

"Aha," said Mr. Pettifer, nodding as if he understood.

NOT EVERYONE STARED. Some of the kids didn't know who she was—they were new or hadn't heard. Very few knew all the details. The teachers would have been told she was in a lockup for treatment. Acting out. Behavior problems. Self-destructive.

It helped that the place hadn't changed. Except for the

tech wing, the school was old, high-ceilinged with dark-framed windows along the outside walls. Classrooms were cavernous and shadowy, filled with small rustling noises, the voices of students, the scratching of pens across paper and chalk on the boards. There were the familiar smells—varnished wood, erasers, pencils, running shoes. Everything still the same.

She could have asked for a different school, but San had been on the phone day after day, bugging her, saying the Dragons wanted her back, just like old times. Jigger hadn't called once, but San said he was still interested. Over the summer she had come during visiting hours, out of place among other guests in her designer clothing, sun-bleached hair and deeply tanned skin. Visit after visit, she had brought Jigger's picture and let Skey hold it in her pale sunless hands. Jigger had sent it, San said, because he was at the family cottage for the summer and couldn't come himself. No, he couldn't actually give her the photo—he only had one copy and needed it back. But when Skey touched his picture, Jigger said he could feel her. He wanted that connection.

Between Skey's hands, Jigger's picture had felt vivid, electric. She hadn't been able to look at it directly, had skittered her eyes around the edges until San took it back with a sigh.

"He really loves you, Skey," San had said repeatedly. "He's waiting for you."

Jigger was the reason Skey had come back, but she kept running from any place she might come into contact with him, as if seeing him would be too much, just the sight of him would explode her into flames and she would be gone.

SAN WAS IN SKEY'S 10:30 calculus class. They sat together and emerged for lunch to find Pedro standing nearby in the hall, waiting for them.

"Heading out," he said.

Fear flicked across Skey, delicate and forked as lightning. "I have an appointment at the Counseling office," she said quickly.

"Skip it," Pedro said. "This is more important."

"I'm supposed to go," Skey protested.

Pedro's wiry body stiffened and the friendliness left his face. "I said skip it," he snapped.

San leaned into Skey from behind, pushing her along. "C'mon Skey," she purred. "Jigger wants to see you. We're just along as chaperones."

Instantly, Pedro splashed a grin across his face and became a different person. "Just as long as Jigger wants us," he singsonged, unloading Skey's books from her arms. Alarmed, she reached for them. "You want these?" he teased, walking backward in front of her. "Who're you kidding? You can't read." His straight black hair threw off light, his dark eyes sparkled like the sequins on San's cheek. Skey gave up on Ms. Renfrew and the Counseling office. She hadn't really wanted to go anyway. She sure hadn't asked for the goddamn appointment.

"Can I at least get my lunch?" she said plaintively.

"We'll buy you lunch," said Pedro. "We're traveling in Jigger's Cafe."

Then they were running down the hall, barreling through a school entrance and across the student parking lot. It was fate, Skey realized, as they approached Jigger's car. Destiny had intervened in order to open this particular car door, slip her into this particular front seat and lock her into place.

Next, destiny slipped Pedro in beside her and scooped San into the backseat with Rosie and Balfour. Then Jigger put the car in gear, and they were off, radio blaring, air heavy with cigarette smoke. The car was old, mint condition, no bucket seats. With a grin, Pedro pressed Skey in against Jigger's shoulder and hip. Jigger yelled a couple of comments to Balfour who let out a howl, his thin face cupping the long sound. On cue, Rosie giggled. Rosie, on the edge of pretty, always trying to make up for it.

Sliding some weed out of his wallet, Pedro lit up.

In the lockup, Skey had quit. The rules said no smoking, legal or illegal. Now she was sucking in the second-hand high like a promise—there was no rule about *breathing* it. But as Pedro moved the weed toward her lips, she pulled her head away.

"What's this?" Pedro asked. "You gone clean on us, Skey?"

San leaned over the front seat and wrapped her arms around Skey's neck, kissing her wetly on the cheek. There was the brief scrape of sequins as she pulled away, then lifted the weed out of Pedro's hand and placed it between Skey's lips. "Nah, Skey wouldn't do that," laughed San. "She wants to die young."

Pressed against Jigger, Skey's skin flickered with live wires. She inhaled, focusing on the smoke as it seared in, then out. With her second inhalation, Pedro gave her some room and San dropped back into the rear seat.

"Burger King?" Jigger hollered. "Or McDonald's?"

"Burger King," came the backseat chorus.

At the take-out window Jigger ordered a couple of burgers, Cokes and fries, then placed the bag in Skey's lap and kicked everyone else out. As if it had been pre-planned, the others headed into the restaurant. "Pick you up in thirty," Jigger yelled through the window and drove out of the lot.

Skey began to edge away, just a little.

"Where you going?" Jigger asked immediately, his voice running through her like touch.

"Nowhere." The word locked deep in Skey's throat, husky, slow.

Jigger turned down the radio. "Pardon?" he asked softly.

"Nowhere," Skey whispered.

"Good." He ran a hand over her left knee, stroking it, and Skey played with the Burger King bag, watching nothing as the car turned down a side street that opened onto a deserted park. Everyone home for lunch. Easing up to the curb, Jigger turned off the engine and left the radio on. Carefully Skey stubbed out her barely smoked weed. If she returned to the lockup looking like side effects, staff wouldn't unlock the doors for her again for a very long time.

The birds were back, flying up her throat and shrieking in her head. What was going to happen now? Would Jigger tell her it was over, everything was over, he could no longer love her after she had done what she had done?

For a long moment they both sat staring straight ahead, watching the emptiness of the park, the bare stripped trees. Then Jigger's arm went around Skey, and a hand cupped her face. She had one brief glimpse of his blue eyes before he began kissing her mouth gently, again and again. Small cries of loneliness came out of her the way they always did. Setting the Burger King bag on the floor, he pulled her in close, kissing and touching. This was the way she had dreamed it would happen, lying awake nights in the lockup, rolling in her bed, moving slowly against the mattress. Imagining, imagining.

Jigger didn't say much, just the sounds he made some-times in his throat, and her name, the way he whispered it to her. Finally, he pressed his face into her hair, and they let their breathing slow. In that moment she remembered every bit of his skin, the way it used to move against hers, the way it had been hers. Pulling back his face, Jigger looked at her. First her mouth—for a long time, he looked at her mouth. Then her nose. His eyes moved up to her forehead, over her hair. Then he let their eyes meet, let her look at him.

He was taller, his shoulders a little broader, but other-wise the same—blond, tanned, mouth wide and full, the familiar grin lines to one side. Everything exactly as she had dreamed it—his face, his smile, his voice. Reaching out, Skey traced his lips. Real, he was not a dream. Waves of relief flooded her. Jigger wanted her, he *wanted* her. Finally, she had found that lost part of herself, here with him.

Reaching for her wrist, Jigger slid up her sleeve and ran a finger over one of the scars. Still a deep red, the scar tissue was puckered in a broad angry mark. Briefly, under his touch, Skey saw the scar open into the original wound, releasing a surge of blood down her arm. Then the blood disappeared and she was back in the present tense.

"It was a long summer," Jigger said.

"Yeah," she said. "It was."

Gently, Jigger pulled her sleeve back down. Then he touched and touched her face, claiming her, taking them back to the couple they were before everything bad happened. *It's like it never was*, she thought in a wash of incredible joy. *It never happened and now it's over.*

"Hungry?" Jigger asked softly. "Let's eat."

CHAPTER THREE

THAT NIGHT SHE WAS trapped in the tunnel of light. Just as in the tunnel of dark, she had to feel her way along these walls by touch, listening for any change in sound that might mean a meeting place and stopping every now and then to trace designs carved into the wall. In the tunnel of light, it was also impossible to see, but it was much worse than the tunnel of dark. Here, she had to feel her way forward with her eyes closed against an intensity of light so extreme that every detail was lost in the glare. Even with her eyes closed, the inside of her body felt completely lit up, her brain a circle of grinding light. Her whole body cried out for relief, some darkness to balance the light.

She had never heard another person in this system of tunnels. It had always been a place of aloneness, and it remained so. Though she had gone to sleep with the rock in her hand, it didn't bring the boy into this dream. Tonight the carvings all seemed to be slashes in the tunnel wall, knife wounds that burned under her touch. She moved onward, alone and alone.

She woke with the headache that always followed the dream of light, the whites of her eyes a faint pink. Terry was working the morning shift and gave Skey's eyeballs a few suspicious glances. So did some of the girls.

"I thought you said we'd share," Ann grumbled at the breakfast table.

"I'm not on anything," said Skey.

"Yeah, sure," snorted Ann.

"Skey, can I talk to you?" Terry called from the office.

Skey dragged her feet. She had already received a lecture for missing yesterday's noon hour meeting in the Counseling office. But she had made it back to the lockup by 4:30, so the staff hadn't been too hard on her. Jigger had driven her, and there had been time to park briefly down the street. He had said he would pick her up at the bus stop this morning.

"Come into my office," Terry quipped.

Skey walked into the mind-reading trap. "I'll go see Ms. Renfrew today, I promise," she said quickly, sitting down.

"Yeah yeah," said Terry. Skey shot her a quick glance. Terry grinned, but Skey couldn't make it to a smile. A pause followed as they sat opposite one another, lit by the fluorescent lighting that seemed to work double-time in the office, while the rest of the unit relaxed in relative shadow. Closing her eyes, Skey found herself in the tunnel of light from her dream, still vivid and burning in her head. With a grimace, she opened her eyes.

"Headache?" asked Terry, watching, assessing.

"I guess," said Skey. "A bit."

"School jitters?" said Terry.

Skey almost laughed. *School Jiggers*, she wanted to say. For a moment she felt him pressed against her, the way he had yesterday afternoon in the car before she had gotten out.

If she could just explain to Terry what it meant to feel his hands again, the way everything in her ran toward his touch. But if she tried, staff would probably stop her from seeing him. Adults were always suspicious of teenagers touching each other. Skey gripped the arms of her chair and focused on Terry's slight mustache. Why didn't the woman wax?

"Did your mother call you last night?" asked Terry.

"No," said Skey.

"First day of school," said Terry, surprised, "and she didn't call to see how it went?"

"I don't know if she knew the exact day." Skey's headache was definitely getting worse, coming at her in sharp white bursts. "Can I go now?" she asked.

"Let me know when you're ready," said Terry, "and I'll let you out."

Skey stood to walk out the door.

"Skey," said Terry. "One more thing. What color are you feeling today?"

"Radioactive," said Skey. Walking to her room, she closed her door.

JIGGER'S CAR WAS IDLING at the bus stop. From half a block away, Skey could see him slapping the steering wheel. Quick sharp slaps. "I thought you said 8:15," he snapped as she opened the door.

"There's a new girl in the unit," Skey said, getting in. "She has problems with mornings. She yells and throws things a lot. It's her hobby. The staff had to hold her down, and I couldn't get anyone to unlock the door and let me out. Sorry."

For a second Jigger stared, then lifted an eyebrow. "Sounds like a real party."

Something twisted in Skey's throat. "No," she said, without thinking. "It isn't. It's a dungeon of shit and puke. The rooms are huge as loneliness, no matter how many girls are there. The music's always playing louder than you can think. The girls spend their time thinking about everything they're missing, and half the time someone's screaming. They're a bunch of losers in there, Jigger. A bunch of losers."

The words left her in a hot rush and she was suddenly exhausted, sitting with her head back and her eyes closed. When she opened them again, Jigger was staring straight ahead, one thumb rubbing the steering wheel.

"I'm not like them," she muttered quickly. "I'm not."

"Of course you're not." Jigger's voice pushed up into a bright artificial cheeriness. "You'll be out of there in no time, and then I'll take you to some real parties." He smiled at her, crinkling his eyes at the corners as if he really meant it. "All right?"

It was some kind of deal, Skey realized, staring at him. Jigger was offering this grin to her as a contract. *We won't pay any attention to the shit*, he was telling her, *and the shit will go away. When we're together, no shit.*

She pulled a tight smile over her lips and said, "Just a short stay at the Holiday Inn."

A brief coldness came and went in Jigger's eyes, but he kept grinning and she kept smiling. Contract smiled, deal closed.

"You got it," Jigger said.

THE GUY SITTING behind Skey in homeroom kept shifting in his desk as if he had spiders crawling up his legs. The way he jitterbugged all over his seat, spinning his pen and whispering to himself, made her want to swat him. Without warning, his loony spiders began to desert him and crawl all over her. Skey turned in her seat and glared.

"What's your problem?" she hissed.

"Huh?" The guy glanced at her and froze. Skey assessed him in one fell swoop: pale skin, freckles, thick red hair. *Very* green eyes. Licking his lips, he began to spin his pen. Skey reached out and put a stop to the Bic.

"What's your problem?" she repeated coldly. She knew what hers was—if he didn't stop fooling around, she was going to explode.

He blinked several times. "I dunno."

Skey kept hold of his gaze. This guy wasn't Jigger, he wasn't a Dragon. He was one of the low-level termites of this school, and she could run him with her little finger. That much was established. "Well," she said in an icy drop-dead tone. "Do you think you could keep quiet for a *couple* of minutes?"

Across the aisle, another guy hunched over a notebook, working on a sketch that was probably obscene. "Ooo, Lick," he said. "Beautiful's talking to you."

Lick licked his lips again. "Yeah, I know," he muttered.

"So, you gonna ask her out?" asked the other guy.

Lick flowered into a rose pink and dropped his eyes. He reached for the Bic, but Skey kept her grip on it.

Your name is Lick? she thought. *You are such a loser.*

Lick gave the other guy a sideways glance. "Isn't she going out with Genghis Khan?" he asked. "I need my balls, man."

The other guy began a high ongoing giggle, and a tiny smile crept into a corner of Skey's mouth. This fidgetty scarecrow, this bundle of nerves, this low-level loser had actually said something interesting. "Lick," she commanded, pulling the pen from under his fingers.

"Huh?" Surprised, he looked straight at her, and she saw intelligent life in his eyes. And nerves ready to blow.

"Give me your arm," she said. When he didn't move, she pulled his left arm flat across the desk and slid up his sleeve. More giggles from the pornographer across the aisle. Uncapping the pen, Skey scribbled on Lick's binder to make sure it worked. It looked frequently masticated.

"Too bad it's not magic marker," she said. Then she wrote SKEY SAYS I MUST BE QUIET IN CLASS along the inside of Lick's forearm. His muscles tensed and he trembled several times as she wrote. The boy was in shock. When she finished, Skey patted his arm softly.

"There, there," she said.

The pornographer gave Skey's inscription a quick glance. "You been told, Lick," he said.

Lick read his arm about twenty-five times. As the bell rang, Skey handed him his pen. Very briefly, his green eyes met hers.

"I will never wash this arm," he said. "You will have to do it for me."

Ms. RENFREW WAS not pleased. Frowning over bifocals and a very large nose, she said, "I didn't appreciate my time being wasted yesterday."

Grim. Ms. Renfrew was grim. Her words were tombstones. A conversation with this woman was a stroll through a cemetery, each phrase appearing on yet another granite slab: *Skey Mitchell, flunked out at sixteen. Skey Mitchell, locked up at sixteen. Skey Mitchell, dead at sixteen.*

"Ms. Mitchell," demanded the grim Ms. Renfrew. "*Could* I have your attention please?"

"Huh?" Pulling herself out of the cemetery, Skey focused

on Ms. Renfrew's nose. It was so huge. A lot of breathing
went on there. "I'm sorry, Ms. Renfrew," she said quickly. "I
didn't mean to forget you yesterday. It was my first day back
and I got talking to some friends."

Ms. Renfrew did not look impressed. Reaching to one
side, she pulled a large stack of books to the center of her
desk. "Well, Skey," she said, "I've arranged for some lunch-
hour tutoring to help you catch up. You will meet with your
tutor on Mondays, Wednesdays and Fridays at twelve o'clock
sharp."

Skey's mouth dropped. Ms. Renfrew nodded grimly.

"We thought we'd leave you Tuesday and Thursday lunch
hours to socialize," she said. "Your tutor is Tammy Nanji. I've
gone over the catch-up work with her. She's a grade ahead of
you and an excellent student, so she won't have any problems
with it."

Skey waved a hand vaguely, trying to break through her
shock. "I can't," she managed.

"Pardon?" asked Ms. Renfrew.

"I can't," Skey stammered again. "Not three lunch hours."
Jigger would be *so* mad. "Maybe one?" she suggested weakly.

"Skey." Ms. Renfrew leaned forward dramatically. "I
realize this is a difficult time for you, but you need to focus
on your studies. This will help you get through it. You're a
bright girl, you did well in junior high. Unfortunately, high
school seems to have been another story."

"I can't," Skey stammered again. "Not three."

"How about you work that out with Tammy?" said Ms.
Renfrew. "She's waiting in the lobby. I'll call her in."

Walking to the door, Ms. Renfrew opened it and beckoned. "Skey Mitchell," she said cheerily, "I'd like you to
meet Tammy Nanji. Tammy, this is Skey."

Skey's neck went ramrod stiff, and she sat staring at the stack of books Ms. Renfrew had left on the desk. She knew she had to focus on something mundane, because all around her the office walls were taking on a harsh white glow. Large gashes were appearing in them. The walls were beginning to bleed, everywhere there was bleeding.

"Skey?" called a voice.

Hands gripped both of Skey's shoulders and she sat deep in a trance, watching the huge nose that had appeared in front of her face. The nostrils moved in and out, in and out. Breathing, breathing, all that breathing. Fascinated, Skey breathed in and out, along with the giant nose. Gradually the office walls stopped bleeding, and the tunnel of light faded. Abruptly, Skey realized that she was rocking, her arms crossed over her stomach. She had probably been moaning. *Shit.*

"I'm fine," she said quickly. "Just fine." Ducking around Ms. Renfrew's concerned face, Skey stood and stuck out her right hand with a glittering smile. "Pleased to meet you," she said.

A dark hand hesitated, then took hers. Behind her glasses, Tammy's eyes flickered uncertainly. "Hello," she said. "I remember seeing you around last year."

Fat. Tammy was quite fat. Even her hand felt puffy. "Oh yeah," muttered Skey, withdrawing her own. She couldn't do this, she thought frantically. She wouldn't last one lunch hour with Ms. Tub Brains. "You want to set a time to meet tomorrow?" she asked, trying for another glittering smile. "In the cafeteria?"

"No need for the cafeteria," Ms. Renfrew said swiftly. "We've found space for you to work here. One of the offices is empty."

Skey ditched the polite act. Crossing her arms, she snapped, "Why can't I get one of my friends to help me?"

Ms. Renfrew cleared her throat. "Tammy has tutored quite a few students," she said coolly. "She has experience. And this *is* one of the conditions of your returning to Wellright Collegiate while you're living in the unit. You agreed to work with a tutor."

"I never heard about it," Skey muttered, though a faint bell was beginning to ring in her head. Tutoring—maybe the principal *had* mentioned something about tutoring. He just hadn't mentioned three lunch hours a week with Tammy Nanji.

"So," said Ms. Renfrew, switching to an encouraging hearty tone. "How about you two girls chat in the lobby, get to know each other, and arrange a time for tomorrow?"

"Yeah, sure." Turning on her heel, Skey headed for the door.

"Skey," snapped a voice behind her. "Don't forget your books."

Reluctantly, Skey turned to see Ms. Renfrew pointing a grim finger at the large stack of books on her desk. With a grimace, Skey shuffled to the desk and hoisted the heavy load into her arms. She was never, *never* going to look at any of these.

Tammy followed her into the lobby. "Do you want to sit down?" she asked politely.

Skey glared at her. The girl was so smug. She probably had an alphabetized list of life goals, a whole Dewey decimal system of thoughts. Now she wanted to invade and organize Skey's brain. Skey was sick and tired of people running her life. "No," she snapped.

Tammy's dark eyes widened. Ignoring her, Skey stared grimly through the lobby's open doors.

"Well, what time do you want to meet tomorrow?" asked Tammy.

"I don't care," said Skey.

"Twelve o'clock?" suggested Tammy.

"Fine," said Skey. Without another glance at Tammy, she walked out of the lobby, into the coolness of the large echoing hallway and the nearest girls' washroom. As she entered, someone came out of a cubicle and left without washing her hands. Skey waited until the creature of filth was gone, then dumped her books on the counter. Grimly she leaned over the sink, bracing her palms against the mirror and waited. Her stomach was on a major rampage; she could feel it churning, throwing itself around like a mad dog. With a sudden surge, it sent a mass of acid gushing into her mouth. It wasn't too bad—she hadn't eaten lunch yet—but she gagged for a while, the heaves gripping her with a satisfying totality, a gargantuan force she couldn't fight, couldn't argue with, couldn't think away.

Finally, it was over. Relieved, Skey spit the last of the acid from her mouth and rinsed the sink. She had some breath fresheners in her locker—they would clear the stench. Darting a glance at the mirror, she let out a groan. Tears had plastered her makeup. Her face looked like your basic, all-around smudge. She was going to have to wash it, then skulk through the halls to the makeup kit in her locker, hoping against hope that no one would notice.

Leaning over the sink, she splashed water carefully onto her face. The water felt good, cool liquid sympathy. With measured handfuls, Skey washed away the noon hour session with Beluga Nose and Dewey Decimal Brain. Then she studied herself in the mirror.

Looks to kill: That was what her father said about her, that was why her mother hated her. Long dark hair, purple-blue eyes, the best kissing mouth in the universe and a body guys mentally undressed and kept chained to their beds. Most girls wanted to be her. The rest wanted to put a noose around her neck and swing her from the nearest tree. Skey knew what everyone did to her in their minds—it leaked out through every word, every action, every spasmodic muscle twitch. When she walked into a classroom, everyone changed, even the teachers. She was a magnet, attracting the dreams of everyone around her. A dream hit list. Most of those dreams were ugly. Real ugly. And the rest were stupid. But she had to live them all out. No one gave her a day off.

Standing in front of the mirror, Skey disappeared into the dark tunnel where nothing could be seen. Immediately, stone pressed against her hand, and her fingers slid into a carved hollow someone had left for her to find. Who had it been? What did the carving mean?

"You all right?" asked a voice.

Abruptly, the washroom reappeared—lights too bright, two skinny minor niners staring at her. Hand outstretched, Skey's fingertips were moving slightly on the mirror. She jerked them off the glass.

"Yeah sure," she snapped, brushing past the two girls.

"Hey, are those your books on the counter?" asked one of them.

"No," said Skey and made off down the hall.

Chapter Four

SHE FOUND A STAIRWELL landing with a window and stood staring out. Windows had always been voices calling to her. Lately she had gotten better at hearing them. Forehead pressed to the cold glass, Skey let her eyes carry her from the white glow of a pigeon's wing to the slate gray of clouds. She slid through the colors of sky, not thinking, not thinking, while a soothing grayness filled her mind and body, slowing things down and smoothing them out. Then she pulled her face back from the window, wiped away the film of moisture she'd left on the glass, and let thought come back.

The first thing she had to do was retrieve that goddamn stack of books. Tomorrow she would have to meet with Tammy, and at least pretend to be interested in what she said. And somehow she was going to have to make sure the walls didn't start bleeding again. If they caught her rocking and moaning too often, she would be tossed inside for good. She had been entertaining her emotions too much lately. That was what her mother called it. "You're entertaining your emotions," she would snap whenever Skey showed the least sign of getting upset. That was probably how she thought of Skey's time on the inside. "My daughter is having an emotional fling," Skey imagined her mother telling her friends.

A week after Skey's arms had been stitched up and her body locked up, her mother had come to visit. She had tapped Skey's right forearm with a finger and said, "This is what *It* gets you." Skey had known immediately what *It* meant. No need to elaborate; she had been hearing about *It* for as long as she could remember. She never used to agree with her mother on the *It* subject, but now she was beginning to wonder. Her mother had no scars on her arms. Her mother wasn't locked up, with wires crisscrossing her bedroom window. Her mother wasn't a loser.

Ditching the gray window, Skey returned to the girls' washroom to retrieve the Eiffel Tower of textbooks.

"I CAN'T, JIGGER," she said.

"Why not?" he murmured.

No one knew, no one knew how her skin sang when he touched her. "You know why not," she whispered.

"What happened to your pills?" he asked, slightly impatient.

"How am I supposed to get birth control in there?" she asked, ducking her head. "No one's having sex in a lockup."

They continued to wrestle gently in the backseat of his car.

"I'll get you some," he whispered.

"They do room searches," she said. "If they found pills, they might not let me go to Wellright."

With a moan, Jigger buried his face in her neck, and they wrapped themselves together. They were parked in an alley near the lockup. She was due back in twenty minutes.

"You gotta let me," he said. "I've missed you so much."

"If I get pregnant while I'm in there, then what?" How she wanted the soft slide of his hands. She had been so careful with pills before, had never forgotten to take them. Just this once, maybe she would be safe. Just once...

Entertaining your emotions. Abruptly an image of her mother's clear, unscarred forearms appeared in Skey's mind. No emotions there.

Jigger started fumbling with her jeans.

"No, Jigger," she protested.

"Yes." He didn't look at her, started to unzip.

"No!" she said again, pushing against his chest.

He pressed her against the seat.

"Jigger," she cried. "Stop. Please stop."

"Skey," he whispered, still pressing close. "We didn't hurt you that much, did we? We were careful, we didn't want to scare you." Blue eyes pleading, Jigger traced a finger across her mouth. "We didn't hurt you, did we?" he repeated. "You just have to get used to it, that's all. I love you, Skey, I love..."

Without warning, Skey's brain took a crazy tilt, swinging deep and round. Her arms came up and she shoved at the weight pressing down on her, shoved until it gave and she could get at the car door, open it and scramble out into the cold November wind. Backing away, she was backing away from the crazy things going through her head, the crazy way that car and the boy in it made her feel.

"Skey." Scrambling out after her, Jigger grabbed Skey's wrist. As his arms closed around her, she scratched and clawed, screaming into the hand that covered her mouth. Suddenly a glare of light lit up all around her. Closing her eyes, Skey stopped struggling and slipped into the tunnel of light in her mind, where the very air throbbed with fear.

Sobs broke out of her and she reached for the nearest wall, fumbling for a carving. *Calm down*, she thought, stroking the cold stone. *Calm down, calm down. Quiet.*

The tunnel of light faded. Opening her eyes, Skey found Jigger still holding her. She was standing, turned away from him, one hand outstretched and reaching toward nothing. In the lengthening silence, they breathed heavily.

"What's with you?" asked Jigger. "You always wanted to before."

"I can't get pregnant," she mumbled, not looking at him.

"My sister will get a prescription," Jigger said quietly. "She isn't seeing anyone. You can use hers. Just keep it in your locker and take it at school."

Some of the fear left Skey. She let Jigger pull her in against the warmth of his body.

"Will you take it if I get it for you?" he asked softly, nuzzling her neck. A deep sigh sifted through Skey. She turned to him, and they began kissing, talking with their lips.

"I just can't get pregnant," she murmured.

"It's 4:25," he said. "I have to get you back to the iron gate."

"The gate to Hell," she said.

"Open wide," he teased.

ONE BLOCK FROM the gate, he let her out of the car and put a squeal on the tires as he drove off. Raising a hand to wave, Skey noticed an ache in her wrist. As she flexed it, she winced. Jigger must have twisted her arm when he grabbed it. Already the skin was beginning to discolor. And her mouth, she realized, touching it. Where Jigger had covered it to silence her screaming—the skin was chafed. She touched it again, longer this time. Was her face going to bruise too?

THE UNIT WAS changing. Schoolbooks deposited on her bed, Skey stood in her doorway, surveying the large room in front of her. Girls were scattered everywhere, eating an after-school snack in the kitchen or playing a game of pool. The largest group had gathered in a tight clump in front of the TV, with Viv in the middle. Only here three weeks, Skey realized, and already the new girl was taking charge.

There had been tough girls in the unit before, but over the summer they had gone AWOL. Their beds had been held for twenty-one days, and then each runner had been discharged. That had left the rest of the girls, the ones who had acted tough on the outside but collapsed into a whimper once they were admitted. Which meant that September and the first half of October had been peaceful—peaceful, that is, for a bunch of losers in a lockup.

But now Viv was here, and it was difficult for Skey to track the shifting hierarchy in the group when she was away all day. Things changed while she was gone; girls paired off differently, arranged in new formations. Battle formations—girls against staff, girls against each other. This week, every girl in the unit was realigning around Viv, giving her jokes the loudest laughs, automatically passing her the channel changer when she sat down to watch TV. Some stuck to her like glue, others stayed far away. Staff kept their eyes constantly on her. No matter what she was doing, Viv was everyone's business.

"Group," called a voice from the office doorway, and groans went up around the TV, Viv's the loudest.

"C'mon," insisted the staff. "All of you." It was Drew, one of the unit's two male staff.

"What do I get if I'm a good girl, Drew?" Viv asked, arcing her voice suggestively. Giggles exploded around her, but Drew kept his face expressionless as he sat down at a kitchen table. Gradually everyone wandered over and chose a seat. Settling into the chair furthest from Viv, Skey went into watching mode. Penny, the unit supervisor, came over and sat down beside her. She was an older woman, her hair a silver gray. None of the girls would ever hit her.

"There has been a problem," Penny said slowly, "in the tub room."

The unit had a separate room for baths. Each tub had its own cubicle and was shared by two girls. The door could be locked from the inside by turning a knob, but only staff had the key to unlock it from the outside.

"One of the cubicles has been broken into," Penny added. "The lock is hanging off the door."

The girls seated closest to Viv were copying her ultra-bored expression. At the next table, Skey could see Ann staring down at her lap and scratching the inside of her wrist. The skin was reddening, going raw.

"It must have happened this morning," continued Penny. "The lock wasn't broken last night."

"Whose cubicle is it?" asked Viv, without losing her bored expression.

"It belongs to Ann and Leslie," said Penny.

"So ask them, why don't you?" demanded Viv.

"We've already spoken with them," said Penny. "Now we're asking everyone. Anyone with information about this should come and talk to staff. Until we find out who did this, only one girl will be allowed in the tub room at a time to take a bath."

A collective groan sounded. "We're gonna stink like cows," complained Viv.

Penny's mouth tightened, and then she said, "Does anyone have an issue they would like to discuss?"

But no one was raising issues without Viv's permission, and she wasn't giving it. Quickly, the group meeting disbanded, with most of the girls following Viv back to the TV. Without a word, Ann got up and began her table-setting chore for supper. As Skey idly watched the other girl count cutlery, she noticed that the inside of her wrist was still red. Them with a start, Skey noticed that Ann's right wrist had also been scratched raw.

A choking feeling grabbed her throat and she turned away. If Viv was after Ann, then Ann could go talk to staff. That was what staff were for. Skey wasn't risking her neck by getting involved with the problems of this place. She was at her old school again, Jigger and the Dragons had welcomed her back, and everything was like it used to be. Like she wanted it to be. In no time she would be out of this place, and then she would forget she had ever been here.

Walking to her room, Skey closed the door and leaned against it until her quick-running heartbeats slowed and she could breathe normally again.

THE SUMMONS CAME around 7:30. Skey was in her room, drifting through *People Magazine*, when Ann appeared in her doorway. One guest in a room at a time, that was the rule. Without speaking, Skey nodded, and Ann sat down beside her on the bed, wrists curled in to hide the raw patches.

"Viv wants to see you in the washroom," said Ann, staring at the floor.

Alarm shot through Skey. "What for?"

"Wants to talk to you about something," shrugged Ann.

"So, maybe I don't want to talk to her," said Skey.

"It's your face." Lifting a hand, Ann scratched at the back of her neck and her sleeve pulled up, exposing the chafed skin. Skey swallowed. It was so raw, it was shiny.

"What d'you mean, my face?" she whispered.

Ann's eyes flitted around the room. "She thinks you're too pretty," she said quietly.

Fear stirred an oar deep in Skey's gut. "I can't help how I look," she muttered.

Eyes once again on the floor, Ann stood up. "I'd talk to her if I were you," she said. "She's been in the detention center a couple of times. For fights. The last time she used a knife."

"What does she want?" asked Skey.

Ann shrugged again. She was one of the girls giving Viv a wide berth. "I'm just giving you the message," she said.

"She's the one who broke the lock on your tub door, isn't she?" Skey said quickly.

"Maybe," said Ann. Turning, she slipped silently out of the room. For a long moment, Skey sat, staring at the empty doorway. Then she got up, knees wobbling, and walked through the unit's open area to the washroom. As she pushed open the door, every girl's eyes fixed on her, but staff continued their priority business of playing Double Solitaire and watching TV. First time she really needed them, Skey thought desperately, and they were as useless as she had figured they would be. Why wasn't Terry working tonight?

Viv was standing alone by the window. Slowly Skey walked toward her, then stopped, leaving several feet between them.

"I've got an assignment for you," said Viv. Built for demolition, she was big-boned, at least thirty pounds heavier than

Skey. The names of boys were tattooed all over her hands and arms—homemade tattoos, the kind you did to yourself after a few beers. No one sober would ever call her pretty.

"You think you're so good," Viv continued quietly. "You think people worship the ground you walk on because you're pretty. Well, your face don't mean nothing to me, got it? You do what I tell you, or I'll cut it. I'll cut your face like you cut your arms."

Skey flicked her a glance of snow-white fear.

"Yeah," sneered Viv. "I heard about your arms. You did a number one job on them, didn't you? Now you can't be a model. Boo hoo. Let's see them. Push up your sleeves."

Skey's arms pulled in, hugging her stomach. "No," she whispered.

"No?" hissed Viv. Obviously practiced at washroom intimidation, she darted into the closest cubicle and flushed the toilet, then came barreling toward Skey, shoving her so hard that her head banged against the wall. Before Skey could react, Viv had yanked up one of her sleeves and started pinching the scar tissue.

"Stop," Skey whimpered, but Viv slammed her into the wall again, and the flushing toilet covered the noise. Light-dark flashed through Skey's head, followed by a vast wave of pain. Viv yanked up the other sleeve.

"Five on this arm, nine on the other," she said. "You really got going, didn't you? 'Cept if you want to die, stupid, you cut down your arm, not across it."

Viv let go of her arms, and Skey pulled them in. The noise of the toilet drained away.

"Please, just leave me alone," Skey whispered.

At the other end of the room, the door opened and a staff stuck her head in. "How about you ladies continue your chat out here?" she said, her voice pleasant, her eyes predatory.

"Sure, Janey!" said Viv, a loud grin on her face. "Hey, you want to play me a game of pool?"

"Think you can beat me?" Janey was Metis, her dark eyes intense.

"I think I can wipe your butt," Viv proclaimed.

Janey held the door open for the two girls, then headed to the office to get pool cues and chalk. That left a moment outside the washroom doors when no one was close.

Taking a step closer to Skey, Viv said, "You bring me something every day."

Fetch and carry—Skey had guessed it would be this. She was the only girl in this unit who attended school on the outside. "What d'you want?" she asked.

"Some weed, every day," said Viv. "Or your face is gonna change radically."

"Skey, you joining us for a game?" Janey was suddenly a few feet away, her voice loud, her eyes intent.

"No thanks," Skey mumbled and escaped to the solitude of her room.

SHE LAY ON her bed in the dark, holding her wrist. It ached in a dull way, like the rest of her life. No one had noticed the blue-green bruises yet—a grab circle and several finger-prints.

Her chest was sore, but unbruised. The back of her head throbbed against the pillow, but her hair covered that evidence. Jigger had left more marks than Viv.

Outside the window, the sky was a deep blue-black full of stars. One star, thought Skey, for every time she and Jigger had made love. No, that was wishful thinking. One star for every time she had thought of him touching her. Just the memory of his touch brought sheer white stars into her skin, constellations that glowed deep within her.

He hadn't meant to bruise her wrist this afternoon, she was sure of it, and she had wanted him to stop her from running away. He knew her better than she knew herself, really, and all she wanted now was his arms around her, rocking her through the rest of her starry life.

Jigger, Jigger, Skey thought, humming a soft note under her breath. She remembered how he had chosen her. It had been the middle of last year. He had been in grade eleven then, one year older, and had dropped into her group of friends like a smile out of heaven, scooping her away from their boring, endless, small-time jokes. Half those kids were still trying to catch their first date. Jigger had taken her virginity almost immediately.

"Absconded with it," he had called it, grinning. It had hurt the first few times but then something had changed, she had felt as if he was showing her secrets hidden in her body, the reason she was alive. He had told her he thought about her all the time, he was never not thinking about her, every moment of her life belonged to him. And she had wanted to belong to him, to his lips and eyes, his voice, his skin. Everyone had watched them together, everyone approved—especially the Dragons, Jigger's gang. They had been like freeze-dried friends, just add Jigger and they were suddenly all over her life, phoning or dropping by to pick her up for a burger. Fortunately they were all good-looking and rich enough, so her mother didn't complain.

Staring out her window, Skey remembered how her mother had watched her new friends with an ugly hunger, as if she was feeding on their laughter, their fast cars and the

jokes they told. Even the jokes they didn't tell—her mother
fed on their secrets too. Whenever possible, Skey had avoided
bringing the Dragons to her home. The only exception she
had made was Jigger, and only when he insisted, when he
wanted to visit her bedroom and do it under her mother's
nose. Then, right in the middle of it, Skey hadn't been able
to shake the feeling her mother was standing outside her
door, listening in the hall and getting in on the rush.

THREE TAPS STARTLED her. With a relieved sigh, Skey realized it was Ann, tapping on their shared wall. The taps
came again. Rolling onto her side, Skey tapped back. It
didn't mean much; they hadn't worked out an actual code.
It was just silliness, something to do when the lights were
out. Something staff couldn't see or hear.

The next tap came low on the wall, then way up to
the left. Obviously Ann wasn't lying on her bed, she was
standing on it. Grinning slightly, Skey got to her knees and
tapped low to her left, then rose to her feet and tapped as
far up and to the right as she could reach. She was taller, she
knew Ann would have to stretch to match it. Almost immediately, Ann tapped back slightly lower, then added a scattering across the middle.

Skey threw out a few low taps, then climbed off her bed
and tapped along the adjoining wall. There was the muffled
squeak of springs as Ann left her bed, followed her to the
corner, and tapped back. After this neither of them moved,
simply stood in the shared corner, tapping back and forth in
the dark. Different rhythms, sometimes louder, sometimes
softer, none of it meaning anything except: *Tap tap tap, are
you with me, stranger? Tap tap, I'm here, tap. Can you hear
my heart beat? Tap. It's me, tap tap. Tap tap tap. Tap.*

Chapter Five

She crept forward, clutching the rock. The boy had been quiet for a while, but sounds could be tricky here—the tunnels wove and doubled back, refusing to give a straight line on anything. Thinking she had lost him, she was moving less cautiously, and almost stumbled over his leg as she came around a corner.

"I know you're there," he said, suddenly at her left.

She stepped back around the curve, heart bulging like a frog's throat.

"You're following me," he said shrilly. "Why can't you just leave me alone?"

She pulled darkness in close, breathed quick tiny air.

"Are you going to hurt me?" His voice went small, almost a whisper. "Who are you?"

"I'm your fairy godmother," she said, trying to speak calmly. "I'm watching over you."

"Bullshit," he exploded.

Her lower lip began to quiver and she sucked it in. The

silence of dark endless tunnels pressed in, going everywhere, going nowhere. "I'm lost like you are," she said finally.

He remained silent, releasing only the soft quick sound of his breathing. Then something erupted in him and he began a regular tapping sound. His foot? His hand?

"I got lost a long time ago," he said. "I don't know the way out."

"Me neither," she said.

"You've been following me for days," he accused. "I mean nights. There are no days here."

"This is the fourth night," she admitted.

"How long have you been in here?" he asked.

"About five months," she said.

"Who are you?" he asked.

"Just me," she said.

He laughed. "Yeah, and I'm just me. You're a girl."

"So?" she said quickly.

He hesitated, then asked, "How old are you?"

"Between twelve and twenty," she said.

"That's specific," he scoffed.

"I don't like Twenty Questions," she said. Carefully, she took the single step that would bring her to the edge of the curve, and they listened to each other breathe.

"You won't hurt me?" he asked finally.

"No," she said. "You won't hurt me?"

"Why would I hurt you?" he asked.

"Doesn't it just happen?" she said.

"I'll concentrate," he said. "It won't happen."

Another pause followed. She stood, thinking about his voice, what a small part of this vast darkness it was. Yet his voice changed everything.

"Do you remember how you got here?" she asked.

"In a dream," he said. "I went to sleep and when I woke up, I was here. I can't remember where I was before, just that I don't want to go back."

"Why not?" she asked.

"Someone's waiting to get me," he said. "A bunch of them. That's all I know. Maybe they're in here too, somewhere in these tunnels. We should keep moving." His voice grew harsh and he ordered, "And keep quiet so they don't find us. They'll hurt us for sure. They don't like girls, you know."

She didn't think there was anyone else in these tunnels. She would have heard a whole group of them, whoever they were. "Would they dream their way in too?" she asked slowly.

"I don't know." His voice rose into a shriek that traveled along the tunnel, reverberating off the walls.

"Let's keep moving," she said gently, hoping this would calm him.

"Don't touch me," he ordered. "You stay on that side and I'll stay on this."

She moved to the opposite wall and reached out a hand to touch it. "What's your name?" she asked.

"Names are secrets," he said, his voice once again harsh.

They began to move quietly, she along her wall, he along his.

"What do the carvings feel like on your wall?" she asked, tracing her fingertips over one.

"What carvings?" he demanded suspiciously.

"The pictures someone carved into the stone," she said. "They're like ideas. Someone was here before us and carved ideas into the walls. This one means rain, I think. A lot of rain falling."

"How could anyone down here know about rain falling?" he muttered.

"Maybe the person dreamed it," she said, tracing the carving again. "The idea came to her in a dream, like we came here."

"No one else has ever been here," he said quickly. "I've never felt any ideas in these walls."

"Just try," she said. "With your fingertips."

"Shut up and be quiet," he ordered. "Or they'll get us."

SKEY WOKE TO knocking on her door. "Yeah yeah," she mumbled.

"Morning, sunshine," said Terry and moved on to Ann's door.

"Yeah yeah," Ann mumbled.

Curled in her bed, Skey lifted the rock to her face and ran its rough surface over her cheek. Warmed by her hand, the rock felt as if it was the dream stroking her, as if the dream had reached through to daylight and was touching her here.

She and the boy had gone on for the rest of the night without speaking, feeling their way along opposite walls of the tunnel. If she stopped to touch an idea in her wall, he stopped too, continuing on when she did. Once he began to sob, whispering, "They're coming, I can hear them coming. They'll get me again, they'll get me and hurt me." Then he began a long complicated sequence of swearing. She had listened without interrupting, sensing that to speak to him then would be a threat; he had forgotten she was there and they were both alone, following parallel trajectories through the never-ending dark.

Gently Skey traced the rock's white markings. She knew nothing about the boy—his name, his secret name. His face. Or the place in which he lived the other side of his life. Was it Timbuktu? Albania? New Zealand? She knew nothing about him, yet she felt closer to him than anyone she saw in the day side of her life.

"SO," SAID TERRY. "What color are you feeling?"

Skey paused, looking out the open doorway. Jigger would be parked around the corner, car idling. Her wrist had stopped aching. "Blue-green," she said.

"Blue-green like the sea?" asked Terry.

"Blue-green like the first day of a bruise," said Skey. She patted Terry's shoulder with her bruised hand, but Terry didn't notice. "See ya," Skey said and stepped out into sky and wind.

"Skey," called Terry.

"What?" asked Skey, turning back.

"You forgot your bus tickets," said Terry.

"Oh yeah," said Skey. Returning through blowing leaves, she took the tickets from Terry's outstretched hand.

"Not gonna get far in this world if you forget your bus tickets," said Terry, watching her closely.

"But Terry," Skey said innocently. "Today all the buses are sunshine yellow, and they're only letting on happy faces."

Terry's eyes didn't leave her face.

Skey turned away. "See ya," she said.

SHE SETTLED BACK into the seat as the car pulled out from the curb, taking her away from Terry, locked doors, scratched wrists and window wire. Jigger's car had always felt like Jigger himself to her—when she climbed into the front seat, she climbed into his body and let him carry her wherever he wanted, cradled by the muffled rumble of the engine, the smooth ongoing wave of the ride.

"I talked to Cheryl," Jigger said over the radio. "She's going to the Orifice today to get your pills." "Orifice" was Jigger's term for the Family Planning Clinic. "You'll get them tomorrow morning," he added, giving a heartfelt groan. "They ever let you out of that place at night?"

"I can ask," Skey said. "But I'd have an early curfew."

"Real prison, eh?" he grunted.

"Dungeon of shit and puke, like I told you," she said lightly. "Hey?"

"Hey?" he repeated, quirking an eyebrow at her.

"Got any weed you can spare?" she asked, giving him her most entrancing smile.

"*Before* school?!" He gave her a stern glance.

"For tonight," she said, sliding in against him. "In my prison cell. I'll stare at the bars on my window, suck in deep, relax and think of you." Skey kissed the pulse in his throat, feeling it quicken.

"What time?" he asked, his voice growing husky.

"Lights out at 9:30," said Skey. "Light up at 9:45."

"And you'll be thinking of me?" he asked.

"Uh-huh," she promised.

He stopped for a red light. "Then 9:45," he said and kissed her. "I'll light up and think of you. Check the glove compartment."

Skey opened the glove compartment and slid some rolled-up weed into her pencil case, then added a pack of matches—they would get her extra points with Viv. With a sigh, she settled against Jigger's shoulder. The day's first problem had been solved and it wasn't even 8:30.

"Oh," she said, suddenly remembering. "I have to meet my tutor for lunch." She held her breath, waiting. Was Jigger going to get mad?

"What do they think, you're gonna be—a university professor?" He didn't seem to be angry, just irritated, his fingers tapping rapidly against the steering wheel.

"I guess they think I need extra ABCs." Skey snuggled closer. "Why don't you turn down that street?" she said, pointing. "We've got fifteen minutes, don't we?"

"You got it," he said, his voice growing husky again.

She closed her eyes and rode the car's smooth turn as if they were going anywhere, Jigger could take her anywhere she wanted. The turn was so smooth, it was almost like traveling under a summer sky in the middle of a blue afternoon, with nothing to do. She just had to close her eyes, settle back into his body, and her dreams would take them there.

TAMMY HAD GOTTEN there first. When Skey arrived, she saw her tutor sitting at a table in the empty office, textbooks stacked in a neat skyscraper and surveying her empire with a satisfied expression. Drooping under her own armload of books, Skey stood in the Counseling office lobby and watched the other girl. What on earth could possess a teenage girl to *volunteer* to tutor another teenage girl? That meant reading and completing homework assignments that weren't even her own. Who was Tammy Nanji—the next Mother Teresa? If she thought Skey was a leper begging for a cure, she had another thing coming.

Skey walked slowly into the office, keeping her gaze directly on Tammy. Just as directly, Tammy eyed her back. Choosing a chair opposite, Skey sat down and the girls continued to watch each other in silence. Behind her thick glasses, Tammy's enlarged eyes were very determined. Skey had thought she would be able to stare her down easily, but Tammy's gaze held. As the silence between them lengthened, the air grew dark and a tunnel began to take shape around Skey. Determinedly she fought it off, digging her fingernails into her palms, shaking her head and swallowing hard.

"So, what's up, Doc?" she asked, giving in first, her eyes flicking away from Tammy's, then back again.

Tammy didn't blink. "What do you want to do?" she asked calmly.

Skey shrugged. "Whatever," she said.

"What are you having problems with?" asked Tammy.

"I'm not having problems," said Skey.

Another silence began, bringing a second stare fight. Tammy took a long deep breath.

"I feel an incredible need to piss," she said, getting to her feet. "I'll be back in five minutes. If you're here, we can get to work. I'd suggest Algebra. If you're not here, I guess that means I've got free lunch hours until they find someone who wants help." She leaned forward and added, "Whoopee." Then she walked out.

The room was suddenly full of wings, panic swooping in from every direction. The breathing, it was the breathing that got Skey—the way air faded so she couldn't get any. Sliding her hand into her pocket, she touched the rock. Immediately there was darkness, the boy sitting next to her, his breathing slow, even.

"You're here again," he said.

She paced her breathing down to his.

"I can tell when you're coming in from the other side," he said. "The air changes. There's an electric tingle."

"Positive vibes?" she asked.

"It's a buzz," he said. "Somewhere between blue and green."

Alarm jerked through her. "You can see me?" she asked.

"No," he said. "It's just a feeling—the way blue-green feels. Not a happy camper."

"First day of a bruise," she said softly.

"Something like that," he agreed.

"What do you do," she asked, "when you've pissed someone off? It's someone you don't like much and you wouldn't care, except she has some power over you and you have to make up."

"How old is she?" he asked.

"Seventeen, I think," she said.

"Bribery," he said immediately. "Something illegal works best."

"Not with her," she said emphatically.

"Then grovel," he said. "They like it when you grovel."

"How do you grovel?" she asked.

"My particular style?" he said. "I wimp out. Beg, whine, whimper. I'm a Class A groveler. As in a groveler without class."

"I can't do it," she said decidedly. "Not with her."

"Why not?" he asked.

"I grovel all day, every day of my life," she said. "My whole life is one long grovel."

He went into a thinking pause, then said, "How much power does she have?"

From a long way off, she heard Tammy re-enter the office. "I take your point," she muttered and returned to the well-lit room, blinking as her eyes adjusted to the fluorescent light.

"Have a good piss?" asked Skey.

"It was fine," Tammy said, sitting down.

"Did you wash your hands?" asked Skey.

Tammy smiled a little. "Yes."

"Algebra would be fine," Skey said.

THE DESKS IN SKEY'S English class were arranged in two half circles, facing the front. Ms. Fleck, the teacher, had decided upon an alphabetical seating plan, telling the class it was more democratic because it broke up cliques and encouraged new relationships. Skey thought it was stupid. San and Trevor were trapped five desks apart in the back row and Skey's seat was at one end of the front. Beside her sat Brenda Murdoch, alias Miss Upchuck because of frequent gagging noises she made in washroom cubicles. At the other end of the first row, directly opposite Skey, sat the loser from her homeroom, Elwin Serkowski. Alias Lick.

He hadn't washed his arm and was keeping his left sleeve pushed up. Every now and then his eyes would flick over her writing and shoot toward her, as if he was continually startled at this tiny connection between them, her touch still on his skin. If their eyes happened to meet, he blushed furiously and ducked his head. Every twenty seconds, he licked his lips. Skey wanted to donate some Lypsyl to the future of his mouth, soften his first kiss for the lucky girl.

For something to do, she watched him. If he wasn't spinning his pen, he was tapping a finger or bouncing a knee. His lips moved constantly as he talked soundlessly to himself, and she could almost hear the whine in his head driving him insane. He probably heard mysterious voices talking about alien invasions or the next apocalypse. Whatever disaster was approaching the human race, Lick would know about it well ahead of everyone else. Every nerve in his body was radar scanning for danger, just like hers. What separated them, what made Lick the loser and Skey the success, was that he advertised it. She sat absolutely still. No one saw her fidget, gulp and swallow every five seconds.

It was Wednesday afternoon, just after Skey's first session with Tammy Nanji. Class hadn't started, San and Trevor hadn't shown yet and most of the students were milling around, talking. Drifting to her desk, Skey deposited her books. Beside her, Brenda sat reading *The Guide to Nutritious Dieting*. A member of the Cafeteria Board of Directors, it was Brenda's personal goal to delete every donut, French fry and greasy hamburger that was stuffed down a student's throat. Last year she had started a petition for a salad bar. No one had signed.

"Where'd you get that, the Book of the Month Club?" Skey asked vaguely as she scanned the room for someone of interest.

Brenda straightened eagerly. "I'm researching vegetarian menus," she said. "You know—yogurt, cottage cheese, the kind of food you need to diet properly. How are you supposed to keep thin with the crap they feed you here? You ought to be interested in this. A couple of us are meeting Tuesday and Thursday lunch hours to work out a plan. Want to come?"

"Can I bring my boyfriend?" asked Skey, but she didn't listen to Brenda's reply. Her gaze had settled on Lick. Turned around in his desk, he was talking to some guys in the back row, his right knee jitterbugging as if it was trapped in the fifties. Feeling very intent, Skey walked over to his desk, sat down on it, and tapped his shoulder. Startled, Lick spun around so quickly that he lurched forward. Skey had to put out a hand to stop his face from implanting itself into a vital part of her anatomy.

Guffaws broke out around them.

"Hey, Lick, you want to make a meal?" someone in the back row howled.

The shape of Lick's face seemed to glow against her palm, blue-green, like pain. Without asking, Skey knew Lick could feel it too, this sudden strange connection. For a long suspended moment, the two of them sat surrounded by laughter, his face buried in her hand. Then the weird moment of deep meaning passed. Lick pulled back, his face radioactive, dancing his butt all over his seat. The poor guy didn't know where to look. Everything he most wanted was eye-level, sitting on his desk, and he was bursting at the seams. This was exactly the situation Skey knew how to handle. Smiling, she touched his forearm. Lick let out a moan.

"May I?" she asked. Not waiting for an answer, she pulled his left arm across her lap. Kids crowded in, snickering.

"Hey, Lick, you want crisis counseling?" called someone.

"The guy needs coaching, man," said someone else.

"Kiss her, Lick," a guy hollered. "Pull her down and give her."

Using a fingertip, Skey traced the words she had written on Lick's arm and watched his face burn. Every ten seconds, his body gave a convulsive jerk.

"Hey," she said.

His green eyes flicked up to meet hers—the green of an alpine lake, all the inner life fled deep.

"You bored yet, reading this?" she asked.

Staring fixedly at the teacher's desk, Lick shook his head.

"Maybe I can make it more interesting," she said. "Anyone got a pen?"

An array of pens flashed toward her. Skey fingered one after another, rejecting them. "No," she said, "I want red. Anyone got red?"

"I've got a marker," said San, appearing in the crowd.

Skey flashed her a grin and took it. A silence fell on the kids crowded around Lick's desk.

"Now," Skey said in delicate tones. "You promised me you would never wash this off, didn't you?" She paused for dramatic effect, then added, "Didn't you, Lick?"

His body jerked again. "Relax, Lick," she soothed. "This won't hurt a bit."

Uncapping the marker, Skey placed it on his skin, about to draw something no one anywhere would ever live down. But under her touch, his arm began to shake. Glancing at him, she saw he was shaking all over, small quick shakes like a cold dog. Suddenly his bare forearm looked stripped, something hauled out of the safety of the dark into the vicious light of day, and she had trapped it, a prisoner for everyone to mock.

Without speaking, Skey bent toward Lick's face and touched the marker tip to the end of his nose. His eyes crossed as he looked at his nose, then they uncrossed and he glanced up at her face. She watched his fear retreat as he saw the smile on her face. Wary and silent, he waited.

Slowly, Skey drew a huge pair of kissing lips that extended wrist to elbow over the words on his forearm. Then she capped the marker and handed it back to San. Girls giggled shrilly, guys hooted and began making predictions. Motionless, Lick sat staring at his forearm, which continued to rest on Skey's lap. Their eyes met.

"Promise?" he asked.

Skey handed back his arm. "Just don't wash it," she said.

"Never," he vowed. A tiny grin convulsed his mouth.

CHAPTER SIX

WHEN JIGGER TOUCHED HER, she found out what skin meant. Every time he touched her, it meant something different. Jigger touched her, and she found new places deep within that came swimming to her skin to be touched by him. All last summer, she had sat staring through wired-over windows at a world in full bloom, and there had been no colors, the air without scent, absolutely still. Then San had visited, and placed Jigger's photo in her hands, and the colors in his picture had been so intense, they had burned her fingers. Nobody knew, nobody knew how Jigger touched her. "Skey," he whispered, and she came alive in her skin.

When he dropped her off Wednesday after school, he parked half a block from the gate and watched until she passed through it and was out of sight. Then he started up the car, revving the engine heavily as he drove past the grounds. As the sound of the car faded, Skey felt it take some part of her with it, pulling her into the distance to be with him. Colors, sounds, feelings. *Meaning.* Slowly she approached the lockup's side entrance, its heavy wood door so old, it looked as if it opened onto another century. Ringing the bell, she waited until a staff peered through the wired-over window. With a groan, the door opened onto the inside, with its set of stairs leading upward, past Administration on the first floor, Unit A on the second, Unit B on the third and Unit C on top of it all.

After the outside light, the stairwell seemed dark. Silently Skey trudged up the stairs after the staff, listening to the sound of girls' voices and the stereo coming from Unit A. At the next landing, she turned and followed the staff into the entrance hall that led into Unit B. Over her head, circles of light shone from implanted ceiling lamps. The first door in this short hall opened onto the Back Room, a small room into which a girl was placed if staff thought she couldn't handle things on her own. If she went stark raving mad, a girl was taken over to the school and put into one of several padded rooms that were opposite the gym. Viv had already spent time in these rooms, but Skey had never seen the inside of any of them. Continuing along the hall, she passed the girls' tub room and the door that opened onto the office. Here, the entrance hall ended and the unit's open area began. All she had to do now was cross it without anyone noticing her, and disappear into her room.

"Skey," called a voice, and she turned toward the office to see a tall male silhouette standing in the brightly lit doorway. Skey blinked, trying to make out the face. It got so dark in this place that sometimes it was difficult to see the most basic things. Raising a hand, she traced the air in front of her face. Was there a carving here? If there was, would it tell her where she was, what she was supposed to be doing with her life, *why*?

"Ready for our meeting?" the voice continued heartily. "Your mother's waiting."

Abruptly, the darkness faded and Skey saw her social worker, Larry Currie, standing in front of her, waving his usual cheerfulness like a flag. As always, it brought out a savage anger in her, made her want to punch her name right off his lips.

"Yeah yeah," she mumbled. So, it was time for the mother-daughter bonding thing, strengthening the family chains. Fortunately only her mother had decided to attend these meetings. Mr. Mitchell had declared himself too busy to attend his daughter's improvement sessions.

"Just a sec," said Skey. "I have to dump my books." Crossing the unit, she stepped into the moment of relief that was her room. Aloneness descended upon her and she stood staring out her window at the gray-wired sky and the slow-moving elm. Then a shuffle sounded behind her, and she turned to see Ann standing in the doorway. Skey nodded and she stepped in.

"Pencil case," said Skey.

It was on the bed, out of the line of sight from the office. When two girls were in a bedroom, the door had to remain open at all times. Carefully, Ann removed the weed from Skey's pencil case and slid it into her shirt pocket.

"Don't forget the matches," said Skey.

Without a word, Ann headed straight for the washroom. As Skey returned to the office, she saw Larry still standing by the door, watching Ann with a quizzical expression on his face. Skey swallowed the sudden hook in her throat. Had they been that obvious? If staff went after Ann now, she had better be smart enough to flush the weed down a toilet. Tomorrow Viv was just going to have to wait an hour for delivery.

"So," said Larry, as they walked along the entrance hall and started down the stairs, "how's school?" Without seeming to notice, he stepped on and off the stair with the loudest creak between second and third floor. With a slight hiss, Skey skipped the stair. Within a few days of her arrival, she had assessed every stair in this place—which ones creaked, which ones whimpered, and which ones remained silent under the endless feet that came and went, pressing down on them.

"Fine," she replied, following him into the first floor hall and its rows of social workers' offices, each with several filing cabinets of files analyzing how stiffly a girl sat, how long she stared at one spot, when she blinked. For extra fun, dysfunctional parents were brought in and arranged in alphabetical seating plans. Then the social workers got down behind their metal desks and observed the ensuing crossfire: who got hit, who went down, who survived.

"Skey," said a cool clear voice, and she saw her mother standing outside Larry's office, graceful as a figurine. One light kiss on the cheek, the brief scent of Oscar coming and going—Mrs. Mitchell was delicate air, hardly there at all. Eyes narrowed, Skey looked her mother over. So, she was still working out, keeping herself whiplash thin. As usual, the colors of her face were carefully arranged, her clothing chosen to match the decor in Larry's office. The first time she visited a place, Mrs. Mitchell always wore off-white and took careful note of the color of the walls and furnishings. On return visits, she dressed to match the furniture. Skey had figured out her scheme several years ago when they were visiting her father's boss. The wife had ordered new carpet and furniture for the living room and had caught Mrs. Mitchell unaware, dressed in mauve and seated on a chocolate brown couch. Mrs. Mitchell had twitched and jabbered throughout the entire visit, as if sitting on pins and needles.

Larry's office offered quite a challenge to the fashion obsessed—one red-and-blue plaid couch, one lime green armchair, one sepia armchair, a dark brown carpet and orange-yellow curtains. As she entered, Skey saw her mother take a small determined breath and head straight for the couch. Her aqua blue dress called out to the blue in the plaid. They were an exact match.

Skey was wearing a red shirt and jeans. She plopped down in the lime green armchair and watched her mother's headache begin. Calmly Larry settled in behind his desk.

"So, how's school?" asked Mrs. Mitchell.

"It's been fine since Monday," said Skey.

Her mother gave her a long-suffering look.

"How's your golf coming?" asked Skey.

"It's November, dear," said her mother.

"Oh, has it been that long since we spoke?" asked Skey.

Larry coughed delicately. Something lived in his throat, something he was perpetually trying to eject. "You've started working with a tutor at school?" he prompted.

"Yeah, she's smarter than me," said Skey.

"Than I," her mother corrected.

"She's probably smarter than you too," Skey agreed.

Larry let out a heated Gulf Stream of air. "Skey," he said. "You seem upset."

Skey crossed her arms and stared at the dark brown carpet. "I don't need this place," she said. "What am I here for? I don't freak out. You don't see me getting held down or put in locked rooms. I'm not on antidepressants, or crazy drugs or whatever it is you feed the inmates. I've got a tutor now, I'll catch up at school. So why don't you just unlock your stupid doors and let me go?"

Larry settled back in his chair, observing her carefully. "I'm not sure you've resolved your issues," he said slowly.

"My issues," Skey mimicked angrily. "Just exactly what *are* my issues?"

Larry studied her as if she was in a cage and he had all the time in the world.

"You talking about this?" Pulling up one of her sleeves, Skey held up the scars. Larry nodded silently. Mrs. Mitchell turned her head and focused vaguely on the off-white wall.

"I won't do it again," said Skey. "I never even think about them."

It was true. She caught glimpses of the scars when she bathed and changed her clothes, but they simply brushed past the periphery of her consciousness, a slight electric ripple in her brain. Other than that, she never thought about them. The scars were just there, something on her skin. Something she had done once upon a time, in a fairy tale long ago. In another life.

"Something led to it, Skey," said Larry. "We need to know why you're so angry."

"Angry!" Skey's mouth dropped and she stared at him. "Wouldn't you be angry if you were locked up for five months?"

"I meant before you were placed here," said Larry.

"I wasn't angry before I was dumped here," said Skey.

"Then why did you cut your wrists?" The question came from her mother, broad-siding Skey and wiping out her thoughts. Mrs. Mitchell didn't usually join in on the attack, leaving the fancy-ass mind control to Larry.

Skey's thoughts returned. "I thought I'd beat you to it," she shot back.

Her mother gasped. Behind his desk, Larry coughed again, working the animal in his throat. With a hiss, Skey clamped down on the violence that shifted through her, longing to let loose on the two big fakes in this room, the jail-keepers that held the keys to her life. But that wouldn't help her, wouldn't get her out of this place. She didn't want to become another Viv.

Closing her eyes, Skey gripped the arms of the lime green chair and waited. Darkness settled in around her, and then she heard the boy breathing close by. She let out a long string of swear words.

"I know what you mean," said the boy.

"All I want is a day off," she said. "From insanity. Theirs."

"People are pretty partial to their own insanity," the boy said calmly.

"Lock me up and stare at me," she muttered. "Take digs at me, figure out all my problems. They're just as bad, but I'm the one who gets locked up and they're the ones taking notes."

"So, take them for a ride," said the boy. "A tangent."

"A tangent going where?" she asked.

"Anywhere you want," he said.

As she thought about this, some of her tension receded. "Yeah," she said, and opened her eyes. "So," she said, careful to keep her voice calm. "What were we talking about?" Relaxing her hands, she let go of the chair arms and stretched. Then she smiled at Larry, who had his eyes glued on her, his mind doing flip-flops to keep up.

"Oh yeah," said Skey. "Anger. Well, I have a suggestion for something to keep me calm. I want to go out with my friends from school. Friday night, just for a while. You let me out to go to school and I always come back on time, so I think you should let me out in the evening."

"I'm not sure you're ready for that yet," said Larry. "I'd like to see how school goes for a while first."

Skey locked him in a determined stare. "So give me a curfew of nine o'clock."

"We wouldn't consider an independent evening outing like that for several months," said Larry.

The violence was back, rearing through Skey like a scream.

"Your mother and I have been discussing a home visit," continued Larry. "A Sunday afternoon, perhaps a month from now."

Shooting out of her chair, Skey took two steps forward and leaned over his desk. "No!" she screamed, the sound tearing her mind wide open. Then she turned and raced out of the office, down the hall and up the stairs to her room, where she slammed the door and locked herself into the small quiet space. Shaking, she was shaking. Arms tight around herself, Skey paced and whispered, paying no attention to the words that spilled from her mouth—words full of meanings she didn't understand, didn't want to understand, couldn't listen to, wouldn't hear herself speak.

Someone knocked on her door. "Skey?" called a voice.

She paced, watching the gray sky outside her window, calling the gray into herself—the calm, peaceful, full-of-nothing gray.

"Skey," said the voice. "I'm going to unlock this door now."

"Fuck you," she muttered.

With the click of the lock, the bedroom door swung open. Turning away from it, Skey leaned against the window. Gray, gray—the sky was full of calm, peaceful, nothing-

nothing gray. She breathed it in slowly, breathed the deep gray nothingness into her lungs.

"How are you, Skey?" asked the voice.

Skey turned to face Larry and the staff waiting behind him, lifted her arms and pushed up both sleeves.

"Okey-dokey," she said. "No blood, see?"

Tap tap. Tap tap tap.

Skey ignored the quiet sounds coming from the wall. Lying in her bed, she watched the elm's branches lean into the moon, then pull back, lean into it again and pull back, as if rowing deeper into the night.

Tap tap tap.

She blinked, her eyes raw from staring so long at one place. Blinked again.

Tap tap tap tap tap.

Rolling onto her side, Skey stared at the wall beside her bed. Why did she play this game? It made no sense. She and Ann didn't talk much during the day. At night they lay on either side of the wall, Ann pining for home on a northern reserve and Skey longing for a life that was a world apart.

Tap tap? There was definitely a question mark on those taps. A tiny wash of sadness curved Skey's mouth and she made a soft scratching noise with her fingernail on the wall. Without hesitation, Ann scratched back. Skey felt another wash of sadness. She scratched again. Ann shifted until she found the same place on the other side of the wall, and the two girls continued to scratch gently, sadness flowing from one to the other, almost touching in the dark.

NOW, WHEN SHE entered the dream tunnel, she could count on finding herself close to the boy.

"There's a sound when you come in." From the angle of his voice, she thought he was standing on the other side of the tunnel. "A hum," he said. "It goes with the electric tingle."

"A nice hum?" she asked.

"I dunno," he said. "You could turn out to be a real bitch."

He began to move on into the tunnel. The nightie she was wearing had no pockets. Clutching the rock in one hand, she felt her way along the wall with the other.

"Slow down," she said. "I'm in bare feet."

"What for?" he asked.

"I was in bed before I came here," she said.

"You're in your pj's?" Eager interest tinged his voice.

"Down, boy, down," she said. Guys in dark dream tunnels were no different from the rest of humanity.

"Just asking," he muttered.

"What are you wearing?" she asked.

"Wouldn't you like to know," he said.

They moved on through the dark, somewhere between here and there, before and after. Nowhere. Safe from the human race. Running her fingers over the wall beside her, she traced its carvings, still curious about the lines and curves, but they didn't hold her interest as they had previously. The boy, the way he breathed—it felt so close. She traced the pattern of his breathing with her own, matching it, taking it into herself, learning him.

Out of the silence came a long series of swear words.

"What's the matter?" she asked.

"Nothing," he said quickly.

"Why are you swearing?" she asked.

He stopped. She could almost hear him think.

"It's like a code, y'know?" he said. "A secret language of the elite."

"Everyone knows swear words," she said.

"It's not the words," he said. "It's how you use them. The way the electrical current of them passes through your brain and clarifies your perception of the world around you."

Like she had thought, a defense system.

"It's the way you make them your own," he finished. They stood in mutual silence.

"Can we sit down for a bit?" she asked.

"Don't you want to keep moving?" he said.

"What for?" she asked. "We never get anywhere. We'll never get out."

"Do you want to?" he asked.

She thought about it. The thought seemed endless, pulling at her mind, stretching it.

"Why do you come here," he asked, "if you just want to go back?"

"I wouldn't want to be stuck here forever," she said finally.

"That's not the point," he replied.

He sat down, and she moved across to sit next to him.

"What kind of pj's are you wearing?" he asked.

"Whatever you're imagining," she said.

He laughed softly. "That about sums it up, doesn't it?"

"What do you look like?" she asked.

"I dunno," he said.

"Oh, come on," she said.

"I've never seen myself," he said. "I've always just been here, in the dark."

"I could bring in a flashlight and a mirror," she suggested.

"No!" The fierceness of his voice flattened her.

"All right," she said. "I won't. I promise."

Without thinking, knowing where it would be in the dark, she reached out and touched his hand. For a moment his skin rested under her own, warm and slightly sweaty. Then his hand jerked away, his breath rising into an edgy whine.

"Don't touch me," he shrieked. "Don't ever fucking touch me."

Suddenly he was on his feet, scrambling away from her down the tunnel, trailing a long sequence of swear words.

"Wait," she called, trying to follow, but she was in bare feet and had to go slowly. It wasn't long before his sounds faded and she was left standing alone in the tunnel, one of the endless arteries of a great stone heart.

CHAPTER SEVEN

SKEY CAME GASPING OUT of sleep as the pillow was yanked from under her head and jammed over her face. A weight came down on her chest, pinning her arms, and hands held the pillow tight. No arms to fight with, Skey flopped like a fish, her entire body a desperate arc. The pillow lifted slightly, letting her breathe.

"This is a message for you, bozo," Viv said into her ear. "You keep it coming or things'll get worse."

Skey lay motionless as Viv climbed off her, then stood in the doorway, watching night staff move about the unit. There was no sound when the girl left. She was there and then she was gone.

Pulling the pillow from her face, Skey slid it under the bed. Then she lay in the dark, breathing and breathing deep air.

SHE WOKE THURSDAY morning still moving in her bed, crying as she listened for any sound of the boy, some clue as to where he had gone. After tracking him along a tunnel, she had come to a meeting place, but there had been no way to tell which tunnel mouth he had chosen to enter. He had probably picked the third, she the fourth. Some near miss like that.

Outside her window it was still dark, just the beginnings of blue on the horizon. Getting out of bed, Skey opened her door and saw Terry lit up in the office window, removing her jacket. It was just before seven when the morning staff came on shift, the unit still quiet, lights turned low. Drawn by something, the loneliness of the hour or the shadowy cavern the unit had become, Skey stepped out of her dream of dark tunnels into a dream of this morning, its possibility.

"Terry?" she said, approaching the office doorway.

Terry focused on her in surprise. "G'morning, Skey. C'mon in and sit down."

Skey shook her head. There was something about door-ways, standing between places, the darkened unit and the glowing office. "What do you do," she said softly, "when you've lost someone?"

Terry stood, observing her closely. "Depends," she said, "on how you lost this person."

"I think," said Skey, hugging herself tightly, "that I didn't pay enough attention."

"To yourself?" asked Terry. "Or the other person?"

"To fear," said Skey.

"Everyone's got fear," said Terry.

"But in the dark," said Skey, staring at the floor, "fear is quiet. Until you touch. Then it explodes into white fire, and he runs away."

They stood silently under the hum of fluorescent lights.

"Where are you, Skey?" Terry asked finally.

"I don't know," said Skey. "But I know I'm afraid."

"That's something most people never figure out," Terry said quietly.

Skey shifted her gaze to the woman's face. "You always think of something positive to say," she said. "Even to the losers."

"You think you're a loser?" asked Terry.

Skey hesitated. "I'm in here, aren't I?"

A sound came from her left, and she turned to see the night staff coming down the hall to get her jacket. "Oh my god," the woman said, smiling. "You up already, Skey?"

"It's ten after seven!" exclaimed Terry, starting toward the door. "I've got to get these girls moving. I'm working evenings next week, Skey. Why don't we talk then?"

"Sure," said Skey, but the moment was over.

WHEN JIGGER WAS ANGRY, he sat staring straight ahead, radio on loud and slamming his fingers against the steering wheel. Opening the passenger door, Skey slipped hesitantly into the pounding beat, then sat watching out of the corner of her eye as he leaned against his door and stared at her. His blue eyes were cold, his mouth a thin line. What had she done? Panicky, Skey scrambled with her right hand, feeling for something solid. There, she had hold of the door handle. Gripping it tightly, she ran a fingertip over its metal surface, smoothing out the white waves of fear in her brain. When she glanced at him again, Jigger was still leaned against his door, watching her. Slowly he reached over and turned down the radio.

"So who's the guy?" he asked.

"What guy?" she whispered.

"You know what guy," he said.

It had to be Lick, Skey realized frantically. San must have told Jigger about the incident in English. But why would Jigger care about a guy like Lick?

"It was nothing," she said hastily. "He's a really shy guy. He hits laser red in two seconds."

"Sounds like you want him pretty bad," said Jigger.

"I don't want him!" cried Skey.

"Drawing your panting lips all over his body?" sneered Jigger. "Talk about begging for it. Please, mister, please."

Skey lifted an impossibly heavy hand to brush back her hair. "I'm sorry," she said. "I won't do it again."

"Don't even talk to the guy," said Jigger.

"I won't," she whispered.

"C'mere." He held out his arms and she slid into them, his scent of tobacco and aftershave, the warmth of his mouth kissing her over and over until she was sure of his change of mood and let herself soften. Then they were together, that force of heat, skin and mouths sliding down onto the seat, touching and touching.

"I want you," Jigger moaned. "I want you, Skey."

"Did you get the pills?" she asked.

He fished in his pocket and handed her the package. Slowly she fingered the top flap. It had already been opened.

Just checking things out, she told herself. Of course he would be curious.

"We should wait a week for them to kick in," she said.

"Shit!" he said into her face.

"I can't help it," she protested. "It's the way they work. We should wait longer."

"We'll just take our chances," he said. "Here." Taking the package, he popped out a pill and slid it into her mouth. "I want to see you swallow the first one."

She swallowed and stuck out her tongue. "See? Empty. No babies."

"After school," Jigger said. "We'll take the long ride home."

WHEN SHE WAS SMALL, the screaming that had come from her parents' bedroom had been animal. Wordless, sharpened to an edge, her mother's cries had seemed to descend out of the shivering white stars, then had wound their way around Skey's bedroom and closed in. She was an only child; there had been no one to huddle with. The screams would go on, cutting deep into her dreams, and in the morning everyone would act as if nothing had happened, her father distant behind his newspaper, her mother blank-eyed and unfocused, slipping a few more pills. Before he had left for his day at the city's largest hospital where he cut into people, rearranging their inner parts, her father had always performed his daily family ritual—one kiss for his daughter and one for his wife, his lips brief and cold on their cheeks.

Later, her father took an apartment near the hospital, closer to his scalpels and chainsaws, and the screaming stopped. Skey gradually forgot the barbed wire sound, the night cries that had wound around her and cut her open. Now the stars stayed quiet and the air felt wider, full of space. Looking around a room she had lived in all her life, she would think, *How did it get to be so big? There's so much room.*

Her mother lost weight, became even vaguer and watched endless TV. The first time Skey called an ambulance for one of her mother's overdoses was in grade eight. There had been several since. Though they lived separately, her parents had never divorced. When required, her mother still put on her glitter and accompanied her father to social functions. The odd time Mr. Mitchell made one of his rare appearances in the family home, rooms shrank and the three of them wandered the house aimlessly, their brains on automatic pilot, steering clear of minefields.

Don't speak. Don't think. Don't remember. What was I supposed to remember? It's gone now.

HOMEROOM WAS THE usual low hum of voices, the odd wolf laugh. Standing in the doorway, Skey slid her gaze over Lick, glanced away, then back at him again. Wound up like a mechanical toy, he was leaning across the aisle, examining the pornographer's latest sketch. Both sleeves were pushed up to his elbows, displaying her wide red lips with pride.

Crossing to the other side of the room, Skey walked up an aisle and sat in the desk Mr. Pettifer had originally assigned her.

THURSDAY WAS A tutor-free day, so lunch was at Jigger's Cafe. Leaned against the driver's door, Jigger was stretched out along the seat while Skey rested her back on his chest, eating the French fries he fed her. Jigger had a way of purring when they were quiet and together like this, a low contented sound that vibrated through them both. He called it idling. To him, it was a car sound. In the backseat, San and Trevor, and Rosie and Balfour had also paired off. Ten minutes ago, they had ordered their lunches from Harvey's. Now they were listening to tunes and feeding on a side street, while Balfour recounted the latest slasher video he had seen.

"He stabs her...," Balfour had to stop to swallow, "over thirty times, in all your favorite places. She doesn't die until the last stab. It goes slow-mo, it lasts, man. You get to see every one."

"What's it called?" asked Jigger. Skey felt the rumble of his words in his chest, deep and dark, pulling her down. Thin lines of blood opened on her forearms. She brushed at them and they faded.

"Dreaming Dirty," said Balfour.

Jigger tried to feed Skey another French fry. It was dripping with ketchup. "No ketchup," she whispered, and he ate it, then rustled in the bag for more.

"What's that place like, Skey?" Trevor asked abruptly.

"What place?" she asked.

"Your new home," he said. "Give us the scoop."

"Yeah, all those little girls asleep in their little beds," crowed Balfour.

Letting out a squeal, Rosie swatted him. Jigger slid a dry French fry between Skey's lips and she chewed, mulling over her possible responses. None of the Dragons had ever been in a lockup. She could tell them anything.

Jigger answered for her. "It's a dungeon of shit and puke," he said. "Skey's walking out of there tomorrow."

"I drove by it last week," said Trevor. "There were some cute chicks in the yard. You can see them through the fence. That place would be great for the Dragons. Especially at night."

"Oh yeah," moaned Balfour.

"There's night staff," Skey said quickly.

"Even better," said Trevor. "Can you get us in?"

The air grew radioactive as everyone tuned in. Leaning forward, Jigger turned down the radio. Then he settled back, his arm tightening around Skey's waist.

"Night Games," he said. "The Dragons fly."

Night Games was a series of challenges the gang regularly set for themselves. Gillian had gotten extra keys copied from her mother's set, and the gang had been through the school so many nights, Skey had lost count. They had also been in Rosie's church, the bowling alley where Trevor worked and each other's homes, creeping in after their parents had fallen asleep. All they did was raid the fridge and pull small stunts, never anything obvious enough to raise the alarm and get the cops in asking questions. The point was to push the boundaries and become someone else, that dark shadow of self that ran the night side of everything they did during the day, so they could look at everyone else, obedient to the rules of daylight, and smirk.

But the lockup was different. There were the girls. And staff, paid to stay awake and keep watch.

"I don't have a key," said Skey. "It's not like I work there. That place is a safety vault. No one gets in or out without a key."

"So get one for us," said Jigger.

"They don't hand them out to the inmates." Impatiently Skey fended off a French fry. "You guys can't be serious."

"Blood, blood, blood," Balfour sang softly. Giggling, Rosie stroked his buzz cut.

"You're sick, Bals," said San.

"It'd be awesome at night," said Trevor. "Totally new territory. You looked at the place yet, Jig?"

"Not much," admitted Jigger.

"Check it out," said Trevor.

"Yeah, I will." Gently Jigger teased Skey's lips with another French fry. It was covered in ketchup. With a sigh, she opened her mouth and took it in.

THAT AFTERNOON MS. FLECK divided Skey's English class into groups and sent them to the library to research the historical and social context of *The Merchant of Venice*. It was made immediately apparent that there was to be no choice about research partners. Voice remorseless, the teacher listed off, "Group D: Brenda Jones, Skey Mitchell, Elwin Serkowski…"

From opposite sides of the room, Skey's and Lick's eyes flicked together, then away. It was Group D all right: D for Damned.

Skey drifted slowly through the halls with San and Trevor, then joined Group D, which was standing around a library table. Across from her stood Lick, also chained to the moment, his left sleeve pulled down, the big kiss covered. *So what?* she thought, ducking her head. He was just another loser, and it was about time he got the reality message, wasn't it?

Without opposition, Brenda appointed herself group leader. Then she enthusiastically reminded Group D of their assigned topic: *Architecture in Shakespeare's Time.*

Oh yeah, thought Skey. *Buildings.* She yawned.

"Lick and Skey," said Brenda imperiously, "you cover city layout. Susan, you and I…"

Skey went cold as an enormous wave of white fear rushed over her, sucking her upward into the tunnel of light. Everywhere, light stretched without end, malevolent and so bright it seemed to be shrieking. There were words, she was sure she could hear words. *Loser*, the light was screaming, *you're a fucking loser. You cut your arms, you're cracking up. You're CRAZY, you're a CRA—*

With all that screaming brightness, she needed a wall, something solid to press against. Putting out a hand, she shuffled forward, but what her fingers came up against wasn't cold stone, it was soft and warm. Confused, she ran her fingers over the warmth, feeling out something that felt like a nose and a mouth. Was it a carving?

Abruptly the tunnel of light faded, and Skey saw that she was touching Lick's mouth. Frozen, he stood staring as her fingers brushed back and forth across his lips.

Someone giggled.

"Shit," Skey hissed and jerked back her hand.

"Are you all right?" asked Brenda, openmouthed.

"Just tell me where to get some fucking books," snapped Skey.

Fortunately Brenda was a member of the Library Club. "Shakespeare's time period," she muttered. "Let's see. I think it's somewhere in the 900s. Next to…"

"Fine." Turning on her heel, Skey headed for the stacks at the back of the library. American History—973, Chinese History—950, Italian History—945. Feverishly scanning numbers, she slid into another aisle. No thinking; she wasn't going to invest a single goddamn second of her mind into trying to figure out what just happened. If she didn't think about it, it would fade and disappear, almost as if it hadn't happened.

That was it, she thought frantically. It hadn't actually happened. She had made it up, the whole thing was just another crazy figment of her crazy imagination. Relieved at the ease with which she had solved the problem, Skey stood running her fingers over the books on the shelf in front of her. The spines were smooth, their colors dark blue, green and burgundy. Gradually the wild white voices in her head grew quiet, and a deep sigh shuddered through her. *Here*, she thought. She was here, in the library, looking for thick books about Shakespeare.

Footsteps sounded to her right, and Lick stepped into the aisle. With a hiss, Skey focused more intently on the thick books before her. Thick books were easy to handle, they didn't pull tricks, and they always did what they were expected to do. Five feet to her right, Lick stood fidgeting, not quite looking at her. Skey's eyes settled on a title: *Life in Shakespeare's Era*.

"Here's one," she said brightly, pulling it out. Very thick book, must be important. "Hold this," she said to Lick. Placing it in his arms, she went back to running her fingers over the smooth spines, then pulled out another thick book and placed it on top of the first. Lick accepted them awkwardly, his face reddening each time she placed another book in his arms. Finally she turned, and they looked directly at each other.

"Sorry about your face," she said.

He shrugged.

"I faint sometimes," she said quickly. "I've got thin blood. I get dizzy. That's what happened."

"Don't worry about it," he said.

"Well, I didn't actually know it was you," she stammered.

Red winged through his face. "So, I won't get my hopes up," he said thickly. "I just happened to be your social charity project for the day."

No one's eyes were greener. They burned in his red face, holding hers. Skey's slid away.

"My boyfriend says I'm not allowed to talk to you," she said quietly.

Lick's surprise was tangible. "So that's why you sat..." He paused, leaving the words dangling.

"Yeah yeah," said Skey.

"Tell him I'm castrated," said Lick. "Flesh-eating disease. At a very early age."

Skey grinned weakly at the books in front of her. "Have you got neat handwriting?" she asked. "For this report?"

"I've got a computer," said Lick.

He was so skinny. She could brush him into nothing with the tips of her fingers.

"We'll take notes," he said. "I'll key them into my computer. Then we'll edit." His voice faltered. "You could come over to my place if you want."

"I can't," said Skey, giving him a sideways glance. Didn't he know?

"They could run a security check on me," said Lick. "I haven't got a criminal record."

So, he did know. "Your mom would let someone from the loony bin into your house?" asked Skey.

"Sure!" said Lick. He was on a hope surge now, straightening, gaining height.

"My curfew is 4:30," said Skey. "They won't let me stay out later."

"Oh," said Lick. The guy was crushed, so disappointed she almost had to scoop him off the floor.

"Maybe we could work on the phone," said Skey. "I'll give you the number. I get fifteen-minute calls. Staff might let me talk longer, since it's homework."

"Great!" he said.

Crumbs, scraps, he was happy with anything.

"You wash your arm yet?" she asked.

Lick shifted the books to his right arm and pulled up his left sleeve, displaying her dramatic red artwork. "Nope," he said proudly.

Skey touched a fingertip to the lip's center point, where everything entered first. "It was a joke, you know," she said.

"I know," he assured her.

"I mean, don't take it personally," she said carefully.

"Since when did life get personal?" asked Lick.

SKEY HESITATED, then got it out in a rush. "Y'know that guy you told me not to talk to?"

They were in Jigger's car, looking for a place to park.

"Elwin," Jigger singsonged.

"Well," she said, looking out the window. "I got assigned to work on a Shakespeare project with him. The teacher chose the groups."

"Oh yeah." Jigger turned the car into a back alley. He didn't seem all that interested. "Just remember," he said sternly. "*My* body's the one getting your warm and oh-so-loving attention, right?"

"You know it." Skey grinned, relieved. "Tonight, 9:45. I want to remember every second. I need some more weed."

"Bad habit," he grinned. "Help yourself."

Opening the glove compartment, Skey slid some weed into her pencil case. "Um," she said carefully. "While we were working on the Shakespeare thing? I got kind of dizzy and I put my hand out for balance. I ended up touching his face."

"Whose face?" His mind on what was coming, Jigger had already forgotten.

"Lick's face," said Skey.

"Who?" demanded Jigger.

"Lick," said Skey. "That's what they call Elwin. In case you hear about it from someone else, I just got dizzy, that's all."

"Oh." Jigger frowned slightly, then changed the subject to something more manageable. "Where'd you put the pills?"

"In my locker," she said. "I can't take them with me—they do room searches."

He gaped slightly, then said, "Well, don't forget to take them. You're going to need every single one."

They opened their doors onto cold November air, then slid into the warmth of the backseat. They had twenty minutes.

"Jigger," Skey said, hesitating. "What if I get pregnant? The pills aren't working yet. We never had to worry about that before."

"You won't," he murmured, and she had to forget it then, let it go. The universe wasn't going to stop its mad wild spin and change its rules for her. She might as well open to every way Jigger touched her, she so wanted to be touched by him, loved the gentle curve of his hands, the sounds they made together, their heat. Even though it had been half a year, he waited, touching her until she was laughing and begging for it. Then they were together, rocking and rocking, Skey hanging onto him the way she had hung onto her mother's hand when she was small, so afraid to lose the connection, one small bit of love.

"You know the way dragons do it?" he whispered afterward, stroking her face.

"Up in the sky," she said.

"They wrap tails and fly," he said. "They fuck so hard, they leave claw marks all over each other. But they love each other, Skey. They're soul mates. They love forever."

His blue eyes were too intense and she lowered hers, nuzzling his mouth. No matter what he said, he never left claw marks on her. "I'll love you forever, Jig," she murmured.

"When are you gonna get out of there?" he sighed.

"I'm working on it," she said. "You wouldn't believe the very good girl I'm being."

They got dressed and he let her out a block from the lockup, then drove toward it, checking out Trevor's suggestion. As she approached the gate, he passed her coming from the opposite direction, leaned out his window and gave a long wolf whistle. After that, it was difficult to pull her face into its usual lifeless expression as she neared the lockup's side entrance, but she managed. And as soon as she got into the unit, she took a long bath, trying to wash out every baby-making chance, though she knew if one of them was going to get her, it was already swimming around with its radar going, looking for whatever it needed to destroy her life.

HAVING SWEATED THROUGH Viv's supper-hour glare, Skey went into Ann's room and passed her the weed. "Just tell her staff are watching," she said. "I can't pass it to you the minute I walk in the door."

"Yeah sure," said Ann. Lying on her bed, she was surrounded by *Archie* comics and scratching idly at the scab on her wrist. "Want to see something interesting?" she asked.

"What?" Skey turned to go. Even if she and Ann connected during their nightly tapping game, daylight seemed to take the conversation out of things. They were so *different*. Reluctantly she took the piece of paper Ann passed her.

"It's a list we came up with while we were supposed to be working in social studies," said Ann. "Everything we could think of."

Skey scanned the list of sex terms. *Crotchless panties, RU2BC4SEX, 69 rrr, big wanger*. Why did everyone think the girls in here were experts?

"Pretty good, huh?" snorted Ann.

"Yeah," said Skey.

"You got any to add?" asked Ann.

"No," said Skey. "I think you got them all."

"You never done it or what?" demanded Ann.

Skey was rescued by staff. "Skey," Janey called from the office. "Phone."

The girls' phone was in the entrance hall, but before she could pick it up, Janey called her into the office. "There's a guy on the phone," she said. "Says his name is…" She paused, frowning slightly. "Lick."

"Oh yeah." Eagerly Skey moved toward the phone.

"He's not on your approved phone list," said Janey.

"We're working on an assignment for English," said Skey. "It's about Shakespeare. Just a sec." She ran to her room and brought back one of the thick books. "You think I'm lugging this around for fun?" she demanded.

"I'll take his name and phone number and pass them on to Larry," said Janey. "I'm sure he'll check it out tomorrow. Then you can talk with him on the phone."

"I talk to him all day at school!" said Skey.

"I'm sorry," said Janey. "Those are the rules."

Skey stood staring at Janey, her thoughts in a whirl. This was just about Lick, so why was she freaking? Jigger wasn't on her approved list either—they had decided it would be better if staff didn't know about him—but still, Skey couldn't seem to stop herself from yelling.

"You can't!" she shouted, her voice so loud it burned her throat. "You can't stop me from talking to him!"

"It's just until tomorrow," said Janey, stepping closer. "Skey, are you all right?"

"Of course I'm all right," Skey shouted. Picking up the heavy book, she backed out of the office and fled to her room.

SHE CRAWLED INTO bed holding the rock and whispering to it, but it was the tunnel of light that moved in on her that night, invading her brain with its sped-up, ugly scream waves. Here, there was no one. In the grim harsh light, there was no one near. The boy had run from her into the safety of the dark and she had been banished—banished for touching his hand, his fear. Now she was being punished with light—light without mercy, beginning or end.

In the extreme unending brilliance, she couldn't see well enough to find a wall. Sobbing, she sank to the floor and began to crawl, looking for a tunnel mouth that would take her out of this place, any way that would take her out of herself.

CHAPTER EIGHT

AT BREAKFAST, Viv sat with Skey and Ann. Immediately, Terry's eyes zeroed in on them, but there was no need to worry. Viv had been through more institutions than Skey had heard of. She wasn't about to advertise her gold mine. Her chitchat was all blah blah and directed mostly at Ann, but the message was clear. Skey had been accepted. Obedience was making her popular in all sorts of places. Making sure that she nodded at all the expected points in the conversation, Skey ate her usual half piece of toast, counting calories with every chew, and drank some orange juice.

"Gotta go," she said, standing.

"Have a nice day," said Viv.

Pulling on her knapsack, Skey followed Terry down the stairs to the lockup's side door. Eyes narrowed, she watched Terry's hand go into her pocket and come out with the key.

"So, what's the color of the day?" asked Terry.

As the key slid into the lock and turned, Skey glanced at her own wrist. It had darkened to a purple-blue. "Grape," she said.

The door opened onto the smell of sky and wind, the

rumble of staff cars entering the parking lot. It had begun to snow, tiny specks of white blowing by.

"Grape as in Kool Aid?" asked Terry.

"Grape as in gook," said Skey, stepping out. "See ya."

"Have a nice day." As Terry started to close the door, Skey took a few steps forward, then paused. Clichés were not part of Terry's usual lingo.

"Wait," Skey called, turning back. "My tickets!"

The door opened and Terry stuck out her head. "Do you use these?" she demanded, her eyebrows raised.

Skey smiled angelically. "Please don't make me walk," she said.

Terry handed her the tickets.

"I'm getting good at begging," said Skey.

"Comes in useful," said Terry.

As Jigger drove into the student parking lot, Lick walked by, his head bent into the wind. Every bit of his exposed skin was as red as usual, this time from cold instead of heat. Leaning against Jigger, Skey watched Lick draw abreast her window and smiled to herself. That boy, Elwin Serkowski, had a lot of inner heat.

At that moment Lick glanced up, caught her glance and stopped. Under the weight of Jigger's arm, Skey watched him shuffle about in one spot, then lift his head and start trotting after the car. Instant panic gulped her. What the hell did Lick think he was doing? As Jigger turned into a parking spot, Lick came to a halt beside the driver's door and knocked lightly on the window. Skey ducked slightly.

"*Who* is that?" Shutting off the ignition, Jigger stared through his window. "Looks like someone grabbed his neck and had a turkey pull."

Pasting on a polite smile, Lick continued to take up space in Jigger's window.

"It's...um, Elwin," Skey said and swallowed hard.

"Elwin," Jigger singsonged softly, still staring at Lick. Without warning he erupted, shoving open his door, grabbing Lick's jacket and slamming him against the car. Then he leaned into Lick, glaring into his face.

"Jesus, Jig," said Skey. Tentatively she slid to the driver's door and peered out.

"Shut up," said Jigger, without looking at her.

Lick blinked rapidly, trying to hold Jigger's gaze. "Hey," he said quietly. "I'm not worth the effort."

"Huh?" Jigger demanded.

"I'm part of the lowest order of beings," said Lick. "Speck of dirt."

"Tell me about it," snapped Jigger. He jerked the speck of dirt, side to side.

"I mean, if evolution worked on me for another millennium," said Lick, "I wouldn't get close to your body type. It's not like I'm running a challenge to the hierarchy of the species here."

Jigger's mouth twitched. "So?" he said.

"We're working on a Shakespeare project," said Lick. "She has to work with someone. Might as well be with a speck of dirt."

Slowly Jigger relaxed his grip on Lick's jacket. "Okay," he said. "Let's see your arm."

Unzipping his jacket, Lick took it off. Then he rolled up his left sleeve. Goosepimpled with cold, the skin was clean, showing only a faint red smudge.

"The other one," said Jigger.

It surfaced, also clean, pale and skinny. Jigger snorted.

"Get out of here," he said.

Without sliding Skey another glance, Lick pulled on his jacket and left. Leaning against the car, Jigger watched until the nearest school door swallowed him. "What a *loser*," he said.

Relief bloomed in Skey's chest. "Exactly," she said.

Jigger grinned down at her. "He probably doesn't have anything in his pants," he said. "Everything went into his head. You notice how lopsided it is? He's an alien. You want an alien, Skey?" Diving into the car, he pushed her down onto the seat, and they kissed hard, an unexpected intensity flaring through them. "You think those pills work in school parking lots?" he murmured.

"I think Ms. Renfrew is watching," Skey murmured back. "You want to go do it in the Counseling office?"

"You're mine," Jigger said. "Lunch and after school."

"I've got tutoring at lunch," said Skey.

"Shit," Jigger hissed. Pulling his face out of her neck, he hovered over her, tracing her mouth with his fingertip. "Bring everything to your last class," he said. "When the bell rings, head straight for my car. I brought blankets."

WHEN SKEY ENTERED homeroom, she saw Lick draped all over his desk, so relaxed his body seemed fluid. Sliding into the seat in front of him, she turned around.

"You crazy?" she demanded.

"Certified," Lick grinned, his face flushing its usual red. "It worked though, didn't it? He's assigned me as your official chaperone."

"I'm surprised he let you out alive," said Skey.

"I'm a speck of dirt," Lick assured her. "Not worth the minor muscle power it'd take to pulverize me."

"Yeah," Skey grinned. "You mentioned that."

"They're calling my mom today to run the security check on me," said Lick. "Think I'll pass? I told mom to lie."

"Are you a pimp?" asked Skey.

"Not that I noticed," said Lick.

"Drug dealer?" asked Skey.

"I wish," said Lick.

"Any unregistered weapons?" asked Skey.

Lick flushed. "Flesh-eating disease, remember?" he said.

Skey rolled her eyes. "At a very early age. Did you renew your rabies shot?"

Lick gasped. "Doggone it, you need that for a phone call?"

"This is a lockup," said Skey sternly.

His eyes caught hers and held. Something lived in that emerald green—sadness, deep thought. Skey felt heat cross her face. *She* was blushing.

"I know," he said quietly.

TAMMY WAS EATING. As Skey entered the small room off the Counseling office lobby, a rich smell settled heavily into her nostrils. Immediately her stomach let out a loud growl and she dropped her books onto the table to cover the noise.

"Where's your lunch?" asked Tammy, eyeing her.

"I'm not hungry," said Skey.

"That's not what your stomach's saying," said Tammy.

"I don't eat lunch," said Skey. Sitting down, she crossed her arms over her stomach.

"You don't eat lunch?" Tammy stared at her.

"Eating doesn't interest me," said Skey.

Tammy blinked. "What does interest you?" she asked.

"Not much." Skey pointed at the books lying in a toppled heap in front of her. "This sure doesn't."

"That's because you don't eat," said Tammy emphatically. "Half a person's brains are in their head. The other half are in their stomach. You've got to eat to think."

"I think," snapped Skey, tightening her arms over her stomach.

"No, you don't," said Tammy. "You hover."

"What d'you mean, I hover!" demanded Skey.

"You're like a pale dainty creature that floats above the rest of us," said Tammy, pointing upward. "In a pale dainty air current. You float up there and watch."

"That's racist," said Skey, "calling me pale."

Tammy leaned forward, her breath thick with vitamins and protein. "It's not your skin," she said dramatically. "It's your spirit. You're losing yourself, Skey. You're going somewhere, I don't know where, but it's getting farther and farther away."

"Fuck off." Startled tears prickled Skey's eyes. Why could this girl see what no one else did? Skey didn't even *like* her. Looking down, she bit hard on her lower lip.

"Eat this," ordered Tammy, pushing an unfamiliar food concoction across the table. The aroma that rose from it was loaded. "Your soul is in here," she said grimly. "You eat it and you'll get it back."

The gate to Skey's stomach swung wide. *You'll get fat*, her mind argued, but her hands were already moving toward the morsel of life. Eagerly her teeth tore into the creamy texture, and her mouth filled with a spicy taste. She tore out another bite and another. From across the table, Tammy pushed some orange juice toward her. Skey gulped it down.

"That's better," said Tammy.

Skey was flushed, her eyes brimming. "This is so good," she mumbled, her mouth full.

"Uh-huh," agreed Tammy.

The last bit of food disappeared down Skey's throat. With a sigh, she swallowed the orange juice dregs, then leaned back. The gaping hole in her abdomen had disappeared. She felt solid, connected. Whole.

"D'you want me to bring you another one on Monday?" asked Tammy.

"Yes, please," said Skey.

"See, you're thinking better already." Tammy smiled.

ALL AFTERNOON THE food sat in her stomach like a gift, anchoring her. What Tammy said was true; when she ate enough, there was less of the hovering feeling. Her arm felt like bone and muscle instead of a dragonfly wing.

The burps were something else though—onions, spices and flavors Skey couldn't even identify. Then a couple of farts she could definitely identify. They certainly added texture to the class read-a-loud of *The Merchant of Venice*. Brenda was too polite to comment, but at the end of class, Skey grabbed her jacket and books and headed straight for the door. Halfway down the hall, Lick caught up to her.

"You want me to call you this weekend?" he asked breathlessly.

"About what?" asked Skey, her eyes on the school entrance at the end of the hall.

"Shakespeare," said Lick. "We have an assignment due Wednesday, remember?"

"Oh yeah." Eyes still on the door, Skey slowed. "Visiting hours are Sunday, two to four," she said quickly. "We could work then. It's noisy in the visitor's lounge, but…"

"Sure!" Lick beamed enthusiastically, then added, "I'll bring Mom's laptop."

"You have to be on the approved list," Skey warned.

"I called Mom at lunch," said Lick. "She said your social worker called her at work and I passed inspection."

Skey felt another fart coming on. "Great," she said, "see you Sunday," and fled.

JIGGER HAD PARKED in a nearby alley where they could avoid student parking lot traffic and make a quick getaway. Turning into the dirt road, Skey maneuvered an overturned garbage can. Ahead, she heard voices and some giggling. A girl was laughing, protesting that it was cold. Frowning slightly, Skey passed a leafless elm and watched Jigger's car come into view, Rosie lying on her back on the trunk, Balfour holding down her arms while Jigger edged up her shirt. Rosie gave a spurt of laughter as Jigger paused at the bottom of her bra, then slid her shirt up to her neck.

"Jigger," Rosie singsonged.

"Oh baby," Jigger breathed and lowered his face.

With a cry, Skey turned and ran, stumbling on ground that seemed to be throwing itself upward. The air clenched and unclenched like a heart, the blue sky cracked open and white forks of lightning struck everywhere. Houses crumbled, trees fell.

"Skey!" Behind her, she could hear Jigger coming after her. But she had reached the sidewalk and was close to the bus stop, the bus one block away. Pounding down the sidewalk, Skey hit the bus door as it arrived at the stop. The door slid opened and she stepped into the bus's warmth, its smell of upholstery and too many people.

"Don't pound on the door," said the driver. "Next time I won't let you on."

"Sorry," mumbled Skey.

Edging onto a crowded seat at the back, she closed her eyes and settled into the sound of the engine. Down, down, the sound pulled her down. Relief flooded her as she recognized the dark tunnel taking shape around her, its silence and emptiness. For several days she had been trapped in the tunnel of light, but now she was back. Cautiously she began to feel about herself for a wall, trying to remember that she was also on a bus and surrounded by people. No carvings, she couldn't find any carvings. Where had the meaning gone? Desperately she ran her fingers further into the dark, looking for a moon, a star, a running horse—some sign that would tell her why this was happening, why she deserved it, how she had brought it upon herself.

Abruptly the tunnel shattered, wisps of dark scattering into the afternoon light. "Sorry, honey," said a voice, and Skey opened her eyes to see an enormous woman bending down to pick up her binder. "Didn't mean to knock that off your knee," the woman smiled and handed it to her.

To her surprise, as Skey tried to reach for the binder, she found that she first had to tug her right hand out of the inside of her left sleeve. For some reason, she had jammed her right hand in there so tightly that a red mark had appeared on her wrist where the circulation had been cut off. Bewildered, Skey stared at her left arm. What possible signs could she have been seeking inside the tunnel darkness of her left sleeve?

As THE BUS LET her out, Jigger's car pulled up behind it. The bus drove off, leaving Skey on a quiet residential street, with three blocks to walk to the lockup. A single car drove past, then turned the corner. Shutting off the ignition, Jigger got out of his car.

"Skey," he said, coming toward her. "C'mon, it was a joke. Rosie's easy, you know that. She was laughing. Everyone was just having a good joke."

Fighting the panic that reared through her, Skey shifted from foot to foot. Nothing was making sense today, especially her feelings. How many times had she watched the gang roll around in front of a TV, pin down a girl and grade her assets? When it was her turn, Skey had always gotten a ten and earned a few of Balfour's slasher jokes. She remembered laughing too. No one had hurt her, and they had left her bra and panties on. Sometimes they went farther, she didn't like to think about what they had done to a few girls at parties, but those girls had been outsiders, not members of the Dragons. They had been loaded up on booze and pills first, but still...She didn't like to think about it, she didn't. Anyway, that was with other girls, and she belonged to Jigger. No one would treat her that way, no one would cross him by tampering with her status.

"What's with you?" Jigger asked cautiously as he came to a halt in front of her. "Why'd you run?"

Biting her lip, Skey glanced away from him, down the street. The wild fear she had felt in the alley was draining away now, leaving her with a tired emptiness. For a moment she remembered her mother leaning toward her, tapping a slender finger on one of her scars and saying, "This is what *It* gets you." Then the memory faded and she let it go, let go of everything that had just happened—it was all over now and there was no point in getting upset about it, that never got you anything anyway.

Gently Jigger wrapped his arms around her and they folded together, Jigger solid and warm, Skey whimpering and shaky. "I'm yours," Jigger whispered into her hair. "Just begging to be yours. You know it, Skey, you know it."

"I'm just not used to everything," she said apologetically. "In a lockup, it's different. People act different. There's no guys. You forget what it's like."

"I'm trying to help, aren't I?" Jigger asked quickly. "Aren't I helping you get used to things?"

"Sorry," she said. "I just lost it, that's all."

"Rosie's nothing," said Jigger. "She's too easy, even Balfour says so. You're just right, Skey. You give it, but you're loyal. You're loyal to your one guy."

Skey shivered and glanced away again. "Remember when Balfour stepped on his sister's gerbil with his bare foot and killed it?" she whispered. "For a joke? When he's finished with Rosie, he'll cut her throat."

"Don't think like that," Jigger said softly.

But Skey couldn't stop thinking like that. "She goes out with him because she thinks she can't get anyone better," she said. "I'd never go out with him. Never."

"C'mon," said Jigger. "Bals isn't that bad."

"I dunno, Jig," Skey muttered, looking away.

"I dunno what?" He pulled back a little, his eyes honing in, intent.

"I dunno about the Dragons," she said, "and all that. You know."

"You don't want to be with me?" he asked slowly.

"Yeah—you," she said immediately. "Of course you. It's just the rest of it. Night Games. Rosie and Balfour…" She trailed off, not able to find the words she needed.

"You're just tired," said Jigger. "C'mon, it's twenty-five after four. You have to get back, and I have to wait until Monday. See how you're making me suffer? You still taking those pills?"

"I brought two with me for the weekend," she said. "I put them in my bra so you'd find them."

His eyebrows rose teasingly. "Where?" he asked. "In here?"

"Jigger," she said, "we're on the street." They wrestled, laughing as his cold fingers moved inside her sweater and found the pills under her bra.

"Should've put them lower down," he said, tucking them back in.

CHAPTER NINE

JANEY UNLOCKED THE SIDE entrance door. Then, to Skey's surprise, instead of continuing up the staircase, she turned left at the first landing.

"This way," she said, and led the way into the visitor's lounge.

"Why are we in here?" asked Skey, her eyes skimming the empty room.

Closing the door, Janey turned toward her. "I have to do a search on you," she said quietly.

"A search?" Skey's mouth dropped. "You mean a frisk?" she stammered.

"That's what I mean," said Janey, her eyes grim.

"What for?" demanded Skey.

"We have to be sure you aren't bringing anything in for the other girls." Janey held out her hand. "Give me your books and jacket, and I'll check them first."

"I can't believe this," said Skey, her head spinning. As Janey began to go through her things, she tried frantically to remember if she had left anything in her pencil case, then

realized with relief that she hadn't. Freaking out over Rosie
had made her forget to ask Jigger for some weed, and she
had been ditching the bus tickets at school so no one would
get suspicious. Janey wouldn't find anything in her stuff

But what about the birth control pills? Acid nausea swept
Skey. The small piece of foil was still sitting inside her bra,
where Jigger had tucked it back in. How carefully would
Janey frisk her? Would she be embarrassed to feel up a girl's
breasts?

"I'm going to have to search you now," said Janey setting
down Skey's jacket.

Skey took a step back, her face flushed. "Did you find
anything in my jacket?" she demanded hotly. "No. You
haven't got any evidence, Janey. You're just doing this
because you like it. You're a lez, Janey. A lez."

"Take off your shoes, Skey," said Janey with a tired look
on her face.

"You're going to make me strip?" shouted Skey. "What
are you, a pervert?"

"You just have to remove your shoes," said Janey. "You
can keep the rest on."

"My dad's got money," screamed Skey. "His lawyer will
sue your ass."

"This will be a lot easier for both of us if you cooperate,"
said Janey, then moved around behind her. Skey couldn't
believe the moment the woman's hands flattened themselves
against her back. Hot and cold waves swamped her, and she
shook as the hands shifted downward and ran the inside of
her legs.

"Turn out your pockets," said Janey.

The only thing in Skey's pockets was the rock. Slowly
she pulled it out. The rock lay in her palm, gray with white

markings, unbelievably ordinary. Would Janey be able to
see it if Mr. Pettifer hadn't?

"There aren't any drugs in it," she muttered, glancing
sideways at Janey. "It's granite or something."

Janey frowned briefly, glancing from Skey's hand to her
face. Their eyes held, Janey's searching, Skey's blinking
rapidly. If they took her rock, she would lose everything.

"It's just granite," she said again.

Hesitantly Janey reached out and touched Skey's palm,
her fingers passing right through the rock. "What are you
talking about?" she asked.

Skey stared at the warm brown fingers resting on her
palm. She could see them superimposed over the rock,
taking up the same space.

"Nothing," she muttered.

Confusion flickered across Janey's face, and then she
moved on to the next step. "Could you lift up your sweater?"
she asked. "Just to your stomach."

"*Fuck*," Skey whispered. Abruptly Janey and the visitor's
lounge vanished, and the dark tunnel took shape around
her.

"You're in trouble," said the boy.

Skey could feel Janey's fingers running the inside of her
waistband.

"Someone's touching me," she hissed at the boy. "I think
I'm going to throw up."

And then she did. Without warning, Skey vomited the
remnants of Tammy's lunch all over Janey's surprised face
and sweatshirt. Heaving and sobbing, she stood clutching
Janey's mucky arm for support until she was finished.
Then silence took over again, the dark all around, close
as breathing.

"Sounds like you just did a number on someone," observed the boy.

"Yeah," said Skey. She began to smile.

"Feel better?" asked the boy.

"Yeah," she said.

ANN STOOD IN HER doorway, openmouthed. "She frisked you?" she demanded.

"Yeah," said Skey.

"And you threw up in her face!" Ann squeaked.

"Yeah," said Skey.

Upon her return to the unit, Skey had taken a shower in one tub room cubicle while Janey had showered in the next. Now she was sitting on her bed, her body clenched like a fist as she stared out her window at the nothingness of gray sky. With an effort, Skey turned her head and met Ann's dark gaze. At that moment, it hit her—how wrong she had been. She wasn't different from the girls in this place. It had just taken her a while to understand their loud voices, their constantly pounding stereos and the rigid way they held their bodies as they stalked their cage. She was one of them.

"I'd kill her," said Ann.

"I feel like it," Skey whispered.

"C'mon," said Ann. "Let's tell the others."

They emerged into the unit to find most of the girls sprawled on the couches in front of the TV, waiting for dinner.

"Skey just got frisked," Ann said loudly, approaching the group.

Skey watched the girls' heads come up, their nostrils flaring.

"Who did it?" asked Viv.

"Janey," said Ann.

"Bitch," said another girl.

"Like to see her try and feel me up," said someone else. En masse, the group turned and stared at the office.

"She find anything?" asked Viv.

Skey shook her head, and Viv gave her a tight grin. Behind that grin, Skey could feel it—anger like black fire dancing from Viv to the rest of the group. Two more girls came out of a bedroom, and Viv beckoned them over. Now every girl in the unit was huddled around the couches. In the office, staff were grouped around Janey, conferring.

"Skey's been strip-searched," Viv informed the two girls.

Standing to one side of the couch, Skey opened her mouth to clarify, then closed it again.

"We're one for all and all for one in here," Viv announced loudly. "Skey's done things for me, and now we're gonna do something for her. We gotta stick up for ourselves or they'll start doing that to all of us. Got it?"

The girls nodded.

"We gotta show them," Viv said intensely. "Now. Let's turn this place upside down. Get us some blood. Blood for blood."

Getting to their feet, the girls formed a close circle around Viv, and Skey moved into the circle with them, feeling rage pull the entire group into one thought, one mind—a mind she understood now, a mind where she belonged. This was her rage, and even though she had never felt anything like it, she pushed deep into it, calling it to herself like blood and breath. At the center of the circle, Viv picked up a lamp and began to swing it. Quickly, Skey reached for a second lamp that stood nearby, but as she did, something invisible began tugging at her mind, pulling her

away from the lamp, the couches and the TV. Without
consciously deciding to, Skey began moving away from
the rest of the girls, out of their black fury into a different
darkness, where she could be quiet and rest. In the tunnel,
there was only the sound of breathing—the boy's and her
own, separate from the rest of the enraged seething world.
She began to shake violently.

"No," she whispered. "Not blood. No blood."

"Whose blood?" asked the boy.

"They're taking it away from me," she said. "They're
stealing what happened to me and making it theirs. It's not
theirs. I don't want blood."

"Can you get away?" the boy asked.

"I could go to my room," she said.

"Do it," he said.

To her left, the girls had shifted into a half circle and
were moving toward the office, overturning furniture as
they went. Someone kicked at a wall, and a gaping hole
appeared. Without a sound, Skey slid along the opposite
wall to her bedroom door. As she slipped through it, she
glanced back to see Janey standing by the office, watching
her. The staff gave her a quick nod and tears burned Skey's
eyes. She closed her door and locked it.

Through the door, she heard Janey shout, "Girls, I want
each of you to go into your own room and lock your door.
You'll be safe there."

With a desperate sucking in of breath, Skey listened,
but Janey didn't add, "Like Skey did." Almost immediately,
she heard Ann enter the next room. After this, the noise in
the unit continued unabated for what seemed hours. Lying
curled into herself on the floor, Skey shuddered with each
crash and scream. At one point, several bodies thudded

against her door and she scrambled toward the opposite wall, but the locked door held. A little later, she heard a deep male voice yell, "Police!" Things quieted soon afterward, but she didn't open her door. Crouched in the white tunnel, she had wrapped both arms around herself and was rocking intensely. *Nothing is safe*, a voice wailed inside her head. No one could be trusted; everywhere people erupted into sudden violence. How was she supposed to know what would be coming at her next?

Something touched her hand. Startled, Skey opened her eyes and found herself alone in her room, the door still locked, the unit quiet. The sensation came again, someone's fingers pressing lightly against the top of her left hand.

"Are you safe?" asked the boy.

Darkness faded in and she found herself crouched in the dark tunnel, the boy beside her, touching her hand.

"I've been thinking and thinking about you," he said, "trying to pull you in here. For a long time you were just a glow. Purple-blue. But now you're here. I can feel you, you're in."

"I thought you didn't like to touch," she whispered.

The boy squeezed her hand, then pulled away. "I don't," he said. "Especially you. You're like touching a scream, you're all pain. It wasn't easy."

"But you kept trying," she said.

"I'm all pain too," he said.

"We found each other because we're the same," she said. "We're in the same place, aren't we? No one else ever comes here."

"When I ran away from you," he said, "I got lost. I had to feel my way back."

"Did you use the carvings?" she asked eagerly. "They're like a map, aren't they? I haven't figured them out yet, but you must have—they led you back."

"No," said the boy. "There aren't any carvings. I just thought about you—your voice, the way your voice feels to me. That's how I found you."

The darkness was like arms, holding them close.

"Just don't touch me," the boy said. "Not ever."

"No," she said. "I won't. Never."

THERE WAS A knock on her door. "Skey?" called Janey.

"Yeah yeah," mumbled Skey.

"You can come out now," said Janey.

"Maybe I don't want to come out," said Skey.

"I need to know how you are," said Janey. "If you don't come out, I'll have to come in."

Skey let out a groan. Huddled against the outer wall for hours, she ached from head to toe. With a grunt, she pulled herself stiffly to her knees and creaked to her feet. Then she touched the rock in her pocket, took a deep breath and unlocked her door.

Her mouth dropped as she caught sight of the unit. Holes gaped in the walls, tiles dangled from the ceiling and the furniture was in pieces. Several cracks angled across the office window, but the wire had held firm. Beside her, Ann's door slowly opened.

"Holy shit," whispered Ann.

Across the unit, Monica and another girl wandered out of their rooms.

"You four are the only ones left," said Janey. Glancing at her, Skey saw the woman's left cheek was bruised and her sweatshirt torn. A small patch of hair seemed to be missing from her head. "The others have been taken to the detention center," Janey added quietly.

"Are they coming back?" asked Ann.

"They'll be facing charges," said Janey. "We'll see what the judge says. You girls did the right thing. You went into your rooms and stayed out of trouble." She blinked, and Skey saw tears in her eyes. "Way to go," the woman added.

"I was mad," admitted Monica, "but I didn't want to wreck the place."

Skey's knees gave a sudden wobble beneath her. Too much. The whole thing was just too much of too much. Taking a step backward, she turned, about to fade into her room again, but Janey caught her by the arm.

"Don't you waste a second thinking this was your fault, Skey," she said fiercely. "Viv was looking for something—anything—to blow on."

"I told her," Ann said miserably, staring at the floor. "Skey didn't."

"But I told you," said Skey.

"Of course you did," said Janey. "Friends talk to friends. No crime in that."

Their eyes met, and for the second time that day, Skey felt it. Opening—she was opening to the people of this place. But this time it was a different kind of opening; she belonged with Janey and these three girls in a different way.

"I'll help clean up," she said quickly.

"Me too," the others echoed.

Janey smiled tiredly. "First, let's have dinner. It's nine o'clock and I've been hungry since four."

THEY WERE FEELING their way along the tunnel walls, the boy on his side, she on hers. What had happened in the unit was now over, part of another life. She hadn't told him about it—the riot didn't belong with the two of them, here in the dark.

She stopped, her fingers tracing a carving of circles that radiated outward from a small hole. Sticking her finger into the hole, she slid it around the empty space.

The shape of it, she thought. *There's a sound to it. It's the shape of a sound.*

"What are you doing?" asked the boy.

"Come here," she said.

He shuffled to her side, careful to stay beyond touching distance.

"Feel here," she said. "It's one of the carvings. I've felt one like this before. Here, touch it." Pulling back, she waited as he brushed his hand over the wall. This particular carving, she felt *within* herself—deep, dark and curved. It was a groan. The carving told the story of a groan.

"There's nothing here," said the boy.

"Maybe you missed it," she said. "Here."

"Don't touch me!" he said quickly.

"I won't," she assured him. Gently she ran her fingers over the groan in the wall, tapping to show where it was. "Move your hand toward here," she said. "There are circles radiating outward. And a small hole at the center."

Pulling her hand away, she listened as his slid toward the carving. She could feel it in the dark—the exact moment he touched the groan and passed on.

"Nothing," he said edgily. "Why are you playing tricks?"

"You're the one playing tricks!" Panicking, she swallowed heat and salt.

"No one's playing tricks," the boy said wearily. "You're just imagining things."

"I'm not imagining it!" she insisted. "There's a hole here, it goes up to my second knuckle."

"Yeah yeah," he said. "And circles radiating outward."

"Fuck you," she said.

Confusion beat its ragged heart between them, huge, deep and pounding. The boy took a quick breath.

"I won't hurt you," he said, "and you won't hurt me."

Everything stopped as she remembered.

"We promised," he said.

"But you're lying," she stammered. "The carvings are here. You *can* feel them."

"I'm not lying," he said. "You think I don't want to feel them?"

Surprise opened within her.

"You have your carvings and I just get the dark," he said. "How come you get more than I do?"

"I don't know," she whispered.

"Tell me about them," he said. "Tell me what you touch and I'll listen."

No one had ever listened. Not like this. The realization shook her once, violently, then rippled gently, aftershocks.

"Go on," he said. "It'll be like bedtime stories, except I won't start yawning."

So, in the dark, where no one could see her face or heart, she began to run her fingers over the carvings in the wall, telling the boy the stories they brought her.

CHAPTER TEN

THEY WORKED ALL MORNING, clearing plaster and debris, and dragging broken furniture down the main staircase to the side entrance, where a pickup waited to haul it away. A few girls from Units A and C came in to help, and by lunchtime, there was only vacuuming and mopping left to do. Staff ordered in pizza and the entire group sat in the middle of the floor, eating from paper plates and surrounded by silence because someone had kicked a hole into the stereo and smashed the TV.

"How many holes did they make?" asked Monica, and together they counted nine in the unit's main walls, two in the girls' washroom and several in the head of each girl who had been arrested.

"I hate to tell you this," said Tena, a girl from Unit C. "I know how you love this place and all, but today it is not exactly home sweet home."

This struck them all as absurdly funny. Through their howls of laughter, Tena continued sternly. "I mean, look at the way you keep this place," she said, waving a finger at them. "You have to take pride in where you live. Pick up your clothes. Don't jump on the furniture. Vacuum those carpets."

"Clean under your bed," added Ann.

"Take out the garbage," said Monica.

"Patch the holes in the walls," said Skey.

More howling erupted.

"Sweep up between riots," gasped Skey. This set them off again, until they were crawling away from each other, begging for the jokes to end. By the time the afternoon shift came on, the unit had been vacuumed and the kitchen and washroom floors mopped. A large dining table with matching chairs now stood in the eating area, and Ann's clock radio blared from a corner, doing its best to fill up the large common room with its tinny voice.

Janey came in to work with the rest of the afternoon shift. After admiring the cleanup in the main room, she headed into the girls' washroom. Hesitantly Skey followed her in.

"Janey?" she said.

"Hmm?" asked Janey, turning toward her. Since yesterday, the bruise on her cheek had darkened, and there was definitely hair missing from her head.

"I'm sorry I threw up on you," said Skey, her eyes darting to the floor.

"Hey, it was an experience," grinned Janey. "You don't smell too good inside, Skey. Take it from me."

Skey gulped air. "And I'm sorry I called you a lez," she added.

"That's not an insult," said Janey.

Skey blanked. "Oh," she said.

Janey smiled.

"Well," said Skey. "I'm sorry I called you a pervert, then."

"Now, *that's* an insult," said Janey. "Apology accepted. How long did it take you girls to clean up this place?"

Skey's grin came clear out of the blue. "The whole morning while you were snoring in bed," she said.

Giving her an answering grin, Janey stretched and yawned. "I had a dream about you girls working away," she drawled. "Cleaning everything up for me. It was a lovely dream. I really enjoyed it."

That evening they joined the girls in Unit C for a video, crowding together onto couches as staff set up the VCR. Squeezed in between Ann and Tena, Skey had a momentary flash of Viv sitting alone on a bed, in a small bare room with concrete walls and bars on the window.

"How d'you think Viv is doing right now?" she asked.

The girls stopped taunting staff and shoving popcorn into their mouths. For a moment, no one spoke. Then Tena said it for all of them.

"Loser," she snorted.

"THIS PICTURE..." She paused and ran her fingertips over the carving again. In the dark, an image had come into her mind, a memory of her mother at the kitchen sink, looking out of the window as the sun rose into another winter day. Her father sat at the breakfast table, entrenched in *The Globe and Mail*. Standing in the doorway, Skey was watching her mother wipe the clean counter over and over, her beautiful face turned aimlessly toward the window as the gray sky lit up with pink and amber and she saw none of it. The carving in the tunnel wall seemed to move under her fingertips the way her mother's hand had moved across the counter—

meaninglessly, without purpose. As if the day had nothing
to bring her.

"This picture?" prompted the boy.

"My mother never touches things," she said. "This is a
picture of the way my mother doesn't touch. Nothing can
touch her either."

"Or she'll scream and run away?" the boy asked wryly.

"My mother doesn't move," she said. "She doesn't make a
sound. It's as if I was never there at all."

WHEN SKEY TOOK the birth control pill Sunday morning,
she realized she hadn't thought of Jigger in twenty-four
hours, since she had taken the last one. After swallowing
it, she stood for a moment, remembering his hands on the
steering wheel, casually turning his car into an alley for
more of the backseat, the sweat that glistened on his neck as
they made love, the heat that flowered in her groin and legs.
Then the fierceness of that heat, the way it tore her open,
flimsy as paper. All she could do as he loved her was give
out long curved cries of loneliness, even though they were
together, even though he was inside her, even though he
held her gently in his arms and was touching and touching
and touching her.

As SKEY TURNED INTO the first floor hallway that afternoon,
she saw Lick standing outside the visitor's lounge, peering
nervously through the doorway. The room was crowded
with girls and their families, relatives and boyfriends—no
one who looked remotely like him. Even though he was
probably wearing his toughest T-shirt and coolest jeans, Lick
still looked as if he had tiptoed into a lockup to complete
a high school English class assignment on architecture in

Shakespeare's era. When he saw Skey coming toward him, he got a fuzzy look and seemed to go weak at the knees. For a brief singing moment, she wanted to kiss him thoroughly. It would probably hospitalize him for a week.

"I'm going to let you two work in here," said the staff supervising the visitor's lounge. With a smile, he led them to a very small room next to a social worker's office. "Make sure the door stays open," he said. "I'll check on you every now and then."

"Yeah yeah," said Skey.

The room was so small that two overstuffed chairs took up most of the floor space. Sitting down, Skey opened one of her thick books while Lick set up his mother's laptop.

"I was reading this book this morning," said Skey, holding it up. "I've got a bunch of stuff—gables and gargoyles. I couldn't do any work yesterday because we had a riot on Friday, so we had to clean the place up."

She watched the obvious sag of his jaw, enjoying the moment. Lick licked his lips.

"Are you all right?" he asked hoarsely.

"Yeah," she said easily. "I hid in my room while it was going on. What did you do Friday night?"

He stared at her, a slight red traveling his cheekbones. At first Skey thought he was puzzled by her carefree attitude, her ability to brush off fear. Then she thought, *No, he's hurt.* But why would he be hurt? It was the sort of answer Jigger always wanted.

Then she remembered herself huddled against the wall, alone and moaning in fear. Shuddering slightly, she took a deep breath. "When the girls said they were going to riot," she said hesitantly, "I just went to my room. Something…pulled me there. I can't explain it. It was almost as if some kind of spirit did it. Do you believe in spirits?"

"I...dunno," murmured Lick, the hurt slowly leaving his face.

"At first I was mad like the rest of the girls," Skey said, gaining confidence, "but then something seemed to get hold of me and pull me away from them. It pulled me into my room, and I locked my door. Three of the other girls went to their rooms too. The rest trashed the place."

Across from her, Lick seemed to be struggling for words. "What was the...something like?" he asked.

"Like a dream come real," she said. "Not a bad dream. Like darkness reaching into the day. Not bad darkness. Like your mind, the secret part of your mind that lives on its own and only talks to you in darkness and dreams. That secret part of my mind reached into the rest of me and pulled me away from the riot."

Lick looked as if she was touching him with her words, gently stroking his face. "I believe in that," he said. "My mind's always doing that kind of thing to me."

"It is?" she asked, surprised.

"Except I can't remember much of it after," he said slowly. "I'll be sitting in class, or walking somewhere, and this other part of my mind, a secret place like you said, comes up from the darkness. I feel it deep and coming up like a shadow. Then the real world fades back in. I look at the clock and ten minutes have passed. And Ms. Fleck is on Scene v instead of Scene ii, and I can't remember anything I've been thinking about for the past ten minutes."

"Could be just daydreaming," Skey said quickly.

"But sometimes it's hours," said Lick. "I was sitting on a park bench last week and I almost froze, I was there so long."

Wings were beating in Skey's throat, pale dainty wings that wanted up and away. "Do you…" She fumbled carefully between words. "Do you ever dream about tunnels? Dark tunnels?"

"I don't remember my dreams," said Lick. "I have a hard time remembering anything unless I write it down."

Without warning, the staff who was supervising the visitor's lounge stuck his head through the door. "Everything all right in here?" he asked, smiling cheerfully. "Oh, I see you've got your books open. Raring to go, eh? I'll leave you to it." He withdrew, leaving Skey and Lick slumped in their chairs and staring at each other.

"Don't tell anyone," said Lick. "Mom worries enough about me as it is."

"How come?" asked Skey.

A wary look crept into his face. "She just does," he said.

Sensing his unease, Skey picked up one of her thick books. "This one talks about canals," she said. "You ever been to Venice?"

"Nope," said Lick.

"Me neither," said Skey.

"And this one here," she said quietly, "is the sound the wind makes when it moves through the trees, softly, in summer. Singing to the baby in the cradle, telling her things. D'you remember summer?" she asked the boy, tracing the soft wispy lines carved into the tunnel wall.

"I'm forgetting more and more things in here," he said. "I want to forget."

"You don't want to forget the wind in the trees," she said. "Or green. That's the color trees are. First it's the tiniest April green, when the leaves are just whispering their way out of the brown bark. Then the green gets stronger, more like a song, like the trees are singing themselves through June, July and August."

"To the baby in the cradle," the boy said softly.

"Yes," she agreed.

"Then they get…yellow?" the boy asked hesitantly.

"So yellow," she said, "that it's like a woman singing high up. Way up against the blue sky. Then scarlet and orange. Then brown."

"Falling off dead," said the boy…

…SAID LICK.

No, Lick wasn't saying anything. Motionless, he was seated across from her, the two of them caught in absolute silence like flies trapped in amber.

"It just happened," Lick said hoarsely. "Did you notice?"

In Skey's pocket, the rock pulsed. "How long have you been gone?" she asked.

"I dunno," said Lick. He glanced at his computer screen. "The last thing I keyed in was sewer systems."

"That's not much," Skey said quickly. "Just a couple of sentences. I'll back up and run them by you again."

"But what happened to me?" asked Lick, his voice rising. "Did you notice anything?"

"No." Panicking, Skey stared at the book in her lap. What the hell was she supposed to tell him? That there was another world, a dark tunnel, with a magic rock that took them both there? *Maybe*. If she told Lick about it and he didn't believe her, if he *laughed*, it would destroy everything. The boy in the tunnel would run away again, and maybe never come back.

"I've got to use the washroom," Skey said abruptly. "Be back in a minute."

Entering the women's washroom on the first floor, she stood inside a cubicle with her face pressed against the cold metal barrier, and waited for the shaking to subside. First the larger shakes, and then the smaller ones. When her body quieted, she began to breathe again, steady and even. *The mind's secret place*, she whispered to herself. That was what it was, what it was supposed to remain. You weren't supposed to share it with anyone else, not in *this* reality. Secrets weren't supposed to be pulled into the light of day. They were your most tender part, like a name in the dark. She smiled, remembering. The boy in the tunnel had a right to his secrets, and she had a right to hers.

Breathing cleanly, Skey emerged into the hallway, walked past the noisy visitor's lounge and stepped into the small room. To her surprise, she found it empty. When she asked, staff told her that Lick had departed without leaving a message, but when she collected her books, she noticed something written across the top page of her notes.

I was thinking about you Friday night, it said. *I couldn't let go.*

WHEN SHE RETURNED to the unit, Skey saw that new furniture had been delivered—two sofas and a TV. In one corner, Ann's clock radio continued to blare.

"Skey," called Janey as she walked in. "Your friend San phoned while you were downstairs studying."

Alarm shot through Skey. "What did she want?" she asked.

"No message," said Janey.

"Did you tell her where I was?" asked Skey.

"Just that you were studying with a friend from school," said Janey. It was such a rarity to see a girl reading Shakespeare in this place. Staff were thrilled about it.

Stretching out her arms, Janey began quoting lines about hearts being cut out and bleeding, then dribbled off under Skey's blank stare. "I guess you haven't gotten to the climax yet," she said.

"No," mumbled Skey. She hadn't read any of *The Merchant of Venice*. All she knew of the storyline were the scenes that had been read aloud in class. The play had too many words that weren't part of the English language anymore. Who cared about Shakespeare?

"Can I call San?" she asked.

San was on her approved list, but her number was busy every time Skey called. When she tried to reach Lick to warn him, the phone rang and rang into the empty tunnel of her ear.

SHE WAS HUNCHED against a wall in the tunnel of light. Brilliance glared everywhere, blurring the difference between floor, walls and ceiling. When she closed her eyes, the inside of her skull lit up like a hundred-watt bulb, lines of light shooting across her aching eyes.

The carvings here were sharp-edged. She kept cutting her fingers on them. They were the mouths of wild animals, the blade of a surgeon's scalpel, the sound of her mother screaming. The edge of a broken bottle coming closer and closer to her skin.

CHAPTER ELEVEN

JIGGER'S CAR IDLED in the usual place, one block from the bus stop. Stomach churning, Skey stood watching it from the corner, then realized Jigger was staring into his rearview mirror, watching her.

"Hi." Dumping her stack of books between them, she leaned in to kiss him. Something glinted in his eyes, but he kissed her back. She climbed over the books and they cuddled.

"How was your weekend?" he asked.

She told him about the riot as he slid the car into morning traffic.

"Whoa," he said softly. "That is some place. You kick in any walls?"

"No," she said. "Then I'd be at the detention center, waiting for my trial. And jail."

He gave her a sidelong grin. "I guess," he said.

"What did you do?" she asked.

"Nothing much," he said. "Anything else happen?"

"A riot's enough, isn't it?" she asked.

"It didn't take the whole weekend," he said.

"We cleaned up," said Skey, chewing her lower lip.
Jigger's arm slid around her shoulders, his hand on her
throat, measuring her pulse. "Oh," she added quickly, "I
got frisked on Friday when I got in." She explained, drama-
tizing the details of her regurgitation into Janey's face, and
Jigger threw back his head and laughed.

"Anything else?" he asked when she finished.

His arm tightened, her breath came quicker.

"Brenda," said Skey. "She's a girl from my English class.
Sunday afternoon, she came in during visitor's hours, and we
worked on an English project. She's a cafeteria committee
weirdo."

"Uh-huh," said Jigger.

The city slid by, distant as the music pouring from the
radio—words about love, heat and eternity. Jigger steered
the car into a deserted lot. "We've got ten minutes," he said,
turning off the ignition. "Give it to me, Skey. It's been how
many days? You freaked Friday…"

She pressed against him with relief, gladness taking her
as they sweated it out in the front seat. There were so many
ways she could make him moan, prove that she loved him,
she was his, she belonged completely to him. She had never
even *thought* about doing it with anyone else. Afterward, she
stroked his face, kissing and kissing him.

"Do you love me, Skey?" he asked, his eyes close to hers.

"You know I do," she said, her heart clear, effortless and
blue. Still, his eyes watched her the way a person watches the
sky for signs of storm, danger, change.

"School," he said. "Hell's bells, nine AM."

W HEN S KEY TURNED around in her homeroom desk, Lick
flushed a deep tomato red and his eyes darted all over the

room. Tenderness opened in her, she was so relieved to find him unhurt. No matter what happened, she was going to make absolutely sure Jigger never found out about Sunday afternoon.

"Why'd you leave so fast?" she asked. She couldn't seem to stop smiling. "I got your message after you left."

Lick's lips parted and she watched his tongue flick across them. He began spinning his pen.

"Stop," said Skey, and grabbed the tip. As she did, the Bic grew suddenly warm, and the strongest, most incredible turn-on that she had ever felt passed through the pen from Lick to her. Or was it from her to Lick? Immediately they both pulled back, dropping the Bic, which rolled off the desk and onto the floor.

"Hey, what's with you two?" asked the pornographer across the aisle, halting his sketch.

Quickly Skey turned around so that she faced the front of the room. In her pocket, the rock pulsed. Briefly the classroom disappeared and darkness surrounded her.

"Don't touch me," said the boy, his breathing harsh. "You just touched me."

"No, I didn't." Her words felt huge, thick as a heartbeat. "You're imagining it."

"Don't imagine touching me then," he said. "I can feel it."

THE SMALL ROOM off the Counseling office lobby was starting to feel welcoming, a place she could walk into and find herself. It was a new self that waited for her here, tentative and shy like the sky of a watercolor painting, but it was a part of her that definitely wanted something. What that something was, Skey couldn't yet define; she knew only that she had never wanted it before. Maybe that was what made these noon hour sessions with Tammy Nanji so difficult to figure out. Sitting down across from her tutor, Skey tucked in her legs and eyed the food that slid toward her. Rich with savory smells, it looked harmless, but Skey knew better.

"That last one I ate gave me gas," she said.

Tammy's face broken into a wide smile. "Beans," she said.

"I had reggae farts," said Skey.

"I figured you might," said Tammy. "You have to get used to beans, so today I brought you one with hamburger."

"No beans?" Skey asked carefully.

"I promise," said Tammy.

"Do you swear on your mother's grave?" demanded Skey.

"My mother made it," said Tammy. "It's bean clean."

Skey gave it a dubious glance, then lifted the meat pastry slowly to her mouth. As the smells closed in, her stomach opened into a loud roar and she ditched her concern, biting deep into the flaky crust, meat, vegetables and spices that made her head sing. Instantly the animal in her came alive, tearing its way through deliciousness until the pastry had been engulfed.

"That was so good," she mumbled. Staring down at her empty hands, she felt her eyes begin to water. Was she starting to cry? But why?

"I thought you'd like it," beamed Tammy. "In fact, I brought you another one."

"Two?" squeaked Skey. "But I'll get fat."

Tammy leaned forward in her chair. "You are going to turn into a *genius*, girl," she said dramatically.

One complete tear slid down Skey's cheek. "You think?" she whispered.

"I *know*," Tammy said solemnly.

Skey reached for it.

As Skey's English class made its way to the library, she developed suspicions. When Group D assembled around a table and she got a clear look, they were confirmed.

"You're on something," she hissed.

Across the table, Brenda's eyes widened as Lick turned enlarged pupils languidly toward Skey. For once he didn't flush, just gave her a funny little grin.

"Are you going to be able to do any work?" For a reason she couldn't quite grasp, Skey was furious. Absolutely, no holds barred, mind-searingly furious.

"Nope," said Lick, looking at her calmly.

"Just how are we going to get this done?" demanded Skey. "We have to present on Wednesday, in case you forgot."

Waving a vague hand, Lick settled his head onto the table.

"You shit," hissed Skey.

Without opening his eyes, Lick mumbled something.

"What?" snapped Skey.

This time Lick enunciated loudly. "Isn't your boyfriend the school's main supplier?" he asked thickly.

Brenda was getting a great deal out of this conversation.

"How much did you take?" demanded Skey.

Lick managed a few more mumbles, then drifted off to sleep. Still furious, Skey stared at his orange-red head. This had to have something to do with the weird Bic connection that had happened to them in homeroom. She didn't understand it either, but she hadn't dived into chemical oblivion to try to handle it. Picking up her thickest, most important book, Skey slammed it down next to Lick's head. Instantly he sprang erect, a red table-smudge on his cheek. All over the library, students turned to stare.

"Get up," snapped Skey.

"Huh?" asked Lick.

"I said," hissed Skey, "get up." Standing, she reached for his arm and Lick pulled back, half-sliding off his chair. His large pupils met her small focused ones. He stood.

"We are going," said Skey, "for a walk. This way." She made as if she was about to touch him and Lick moved immediately in the direction she was pointing, away from the open mouths of Group D and through the library exit. Out in the hall it was quiet, every other student in class, only a janitor here and there. Tight and tense, Skey strode down the corridor while Lick ambled along at her side.

"Where are we going?" he asked.

"We are going to walk this off," she said.

"Huh?" he demanded.

"You don't get to sit in La La Land while I do all the work," she said.

"Since when have you done homework?" he asked in open astonishment.

Skey's temperature soared. "How many of those stupid thick books did I read to you yesterday?" she fumed. "Half a library? You think I did that for fun?"

Lick snorted. "I know what you do for fun."

Skey shoved him. Immediately he stepped back, his arms rising defensively. Skey stepped back too, then stood staring at her hands. They felt as if they were throbbing with darkness, and when she looked up again, the dark tunnel was closing in.

"You pushed me," whimpered the boy.

She stared eagerly toward his voice, straining to see through the darkness, to see him.

"What's your name?" she asked.

"Names are secrets," he said.

"Don't you remember anything from the other side?" she asked.

"I don't want to remember," he said.

"Yes, you do," she said. "When I helped you, you remembered summer, and sky, and green, and autumn leaves."

"I remember you nagging me," he said.

"Please remember something," she said. "Please."

Abruptly, the school hall faded back in, vivid with light, and Skey found herself backed into the wall opposite Lick. They stared at each other.

In her pocket, the rock pulsed.

"It happened again," whispered Lick. "Blackout."

"You don't remember any of it?" asked Skey.

"No," he said.

A bitter frustration rose in her. "Get walking," she snapped.

"Ms. Fleck will notice we're gone," he said.

"She's marking papers in the classroom," said Skey.

Lick's shoulders caved.

"No fun time for bad boys," said Skey. "C'mon, get your ass moving."

"You left your cattle prod at home," grumbled Lick. Putting out a hand, he began to feel his way along the wall.

THEY WALKED THE rest of the class in silence, then returned to the library to pick up their books. Without a word, Skey left for her next class. How they were going to complete their assignment by Wednesday, she hadn't a clue. Shakespeare be damned.

She emerged from her last class to find Pedro waiting at her locker. "C'mon," he said. "Jigger's waiting."

A blood-red churn started in Skey's gut. "Yeah yeah," she said. "I'm coming."

Pedro played percussion on her locker door while she grabbed her jacket and books. As they began to walk down the hall, he took her arm. When Skey pulled back, he tightened his grip. "Let go of me," she said, but he walked faster, pulling her along. She had to half-run to keep up. Exiting the school through the nearest door, they crossed the street, then turned in behind a large apartment building.

Jigger, Trevor and Balfour stood waiting. Pressed against the building wall was Lick.

Skey dropped her books. "No," she cried, lunging forward, but Pedro grabbed her arm and wrapped her in a bear hug. "Jigger, no," she pleaded, struggling. "It's not sex, it's nothing. Please leave him alone."

"This guy's name is Brenda?" demanded Jigger, tossing his cigarette.

Against the wall, Lick was muttering swear words, his eyes strangely unfocused.

"We were just working on Shakespeare," Skey begged. "I was scared that if I told you, you would hurt him. Nothing happened. Please don't do anything to him, Jigger. Please."

With another incoherent mumble, Lick raised a hand as if feeling for something in the air. Eyes narrowed, Jigger hissed incredulously, then launched himself. Behind him, Trevor and Balfour closed in. After that, Skey didn't see or hear anything except her own screaming. Pedro clapped a hand over her mouth, but she fought until he pushed her to the ground and sat on her. Finally she saw the three boys pull back, leaving Lick crumpled on the ground.

He wasn't moving, and she could see blood. Slowly Pedro got off her, and she began crawling toward Lick, but was abruptly lifted into the air and carried toward Jigger's car. Then she was shoved into the front seat and the car immediately pulled away from the curb. Desperately she twisted around to get one last glimpse, but Balfour pulled her back and slapped her face. Grim and quiet, Jigger drove with the radio off, turning the car finally down an isolated street in the industrial sector. He parked and a heavy silence settled onto the car, a silence torn and tortured by the coming and going of wind.

She couldn't find any tunnels. Though she screamed for them in her head, no tunnels came to save her from this. Softly, without looking at her, Jigger began to speak.

"There's something you've got to learn," he said. "You've been gone a while, so I guess you've forgotten how things are. How the Dragons run things. How we stick together. You forget that?"

"No," she whispered.

"Dragons don't stick with outsiders," he said. "Dragons keep to their own kind. Everyone else is prey. You remember your vow?"

"Yes," she whispered. She remembered it clearly: candles, the dark, the Dragons standing in a tight circle.

"You remember giving blood?" asked Jigger. "How we all became one blood?"

It had only been fingertips, but still her stomach lurched, remembering. "Yes," she whispered.

"We'll overlook it this time," said Jigger. "The way you gave time to an outsider. To prey."

"It was an English project," Skey protested. "We were just…"

"Shut up!" yelled Jigger. "You do school shit in school time, not Sunday afternoons. When's the last time you spent a Sunday with me, bitch?"

Head down, Skey cowered. "You said you didn't want them to know about you," she whispered.

He pulled his voice down with obvious effort, hanging onto the edge of calm. "So you don't go spending the time you owe me with some *loser*," he hissed.

"I love you, Jigger," Skey said. "All my love's yours, you know that."

She sat, trembling as Jigger pulled in ragged breaths on one side and Balfour pressed in on the other. Behind her hunched Trevor and Pedro, Dragons all around, breathing fire, hunting prey.

"You're mine," Jigger said finally. "All mine, Skey. Every minute of your life, every word you say, everything you do, every thought you have in your pretty little *stupid* head—all of it's mine. You got that?"

She nodded.

"More than that," he said, "you belong to the Dragons. To all of us. Dragons are soul mates, they tune together and become one mind. We're like one person here, that's how it works. You belong to Balfour, just like me. You belong to Trevor, just like me. Pedro, just like me. Whenever we call you, any one of us—even the girls—whenever any one of the Dragons tells you to do something, you do it. You got that?"

All feeling drained out of her. Cold, everywhere she was cold.

"I said," Jigger repeated slowly, "you got that?"

She nodded.

"Let me hear you say it," he said.

"I got it," she said quietly.

"Mark of ownership," he said. "Trevor."

At Jigger's cue, Trevor leaned over the back seat, turned Skey's chin to face him and kissed her full on the mouth. She gasped, pulling back, but Balfour's hands came up to hold her head in place.

"Pedro," said Jigger.

Pedro kissed her hard, forcing her mouth open with his tongue.

"Balfour," said Jigger.

Balfour pulled her in, kissing so long and hard she started to choke.

"C'mere," said Jigger and kissed her gently as tears ran down her face. "Skey, Skey," he whispered. "Remember you're mine. I run this pack. The Dragons won't hunt you as long as you do what I say."

"Jigs," said Trevor from the backseat. "It's twenty after four."

"Shit," hissed Jigger and took off in a squeal of tires. Leaning forward, Balfour began to play with the radio dial, and Skey felt the gang ease off: The problem had been dealt with, they were cruising the land and the tunes. Turning into the street that led to the lockup, Jigger parked two blocks from the gate and let the engine idle. From the backseat, Pedro handed Skey's books to Balfour.

"One more thing," said Jigger, turning toward her. "We gave you an assignment. Night Games. Give us an update."

"It's impossible," whispered Skey. Fear whined shrilly in her head. "There's no way I can get a key."

"You get it anyway," said Jigger. "Friday, two AM, you let us in. Give us a kiss."

He bent toward her and their lips met. With a sneer, Balfour dumped her books in her lap, then got out and held the door open.

"Better hurry," said Jigger, "or you'll be late." He smiled at her, the same Jigger smile he always wore. Or was it? Inside Skey's head, something tore sharply. She whimpered and closed her eyes, waiting for the pain to subside.

"See you tomorrow," said Jigger. "Eight twenty at the usual spot."

She slid out of the car, her legs wobbling as Balfour brushed her with his hip. Behind her the engine idled, the gang watching motionless as she walked the two full blocks to the lockup. The black iron gate loomed, arms reaching to take her in. As she stepped toward it, one loud rev sounded behind her, and then she was through the gate and out of their sight.

CHAPTER TWELVE

TERRY OPENED THE SIDE ENTRANCE door and gave Skey a wide grin. "So," she said. "What color are you fee—"

Stepping inside, Skey leaned against the wall. She felt dizzy. Her face was smudged with tears and her jacket torn.

"What happened?" asked Terry.

"The bus was crowded," mumbled Skey. "This guy kept grabbing me. I *hate* it when guys grab me. I *hate* it."

Terry made as if to pat her arm, but Skey flinched. Mind racing, she tried to figure out how to fend off all possible questions. "I punched him before I got off," she said quickly. "In the gut. He tore my jacket, but I got him back."

"C'mon up to the unit," Terry said comfortingly, "and I'll make you some cranberry tea."

The staircase seemed longer than usual. At the second landing, darkness came at her in a swoop, and she grabbed Terry's arm for support.

"I'm putting you to bed," said Terry, pressing a hand to Skey's forehead. "You feel warmish. Go put on your pj's, and I'll bring you that tea."

Gratefully, Skey crossed the unit and closed her door. Then she turned on her radio. Only one and a half songs and Lick was the main news item. "Police are investigating the beating of a male teen by peers at Wellright Collegiate late this afternoon," said the announcer. "The victim was found unconscious and bleeding and was taken to hospital where he is thought to be in critical condition. His name has not been released. This incident may be connected to a string of gay-bashing incidents in the city..."

"No," Skey whispered. Leaning against her window, she watched the elm's thin branches shift with the wind. Each branch moved differently, the inside of her head blowing in a thousand different directions. A knock sounded on her door and she switched off her radio.

"You're supposed to be in bed," said Terry, opening the door. "It's cold by that window."

Skey slid listlessly between the sheets. "What does critical condition mean?" she asked into her pillow.

"Now you're not *that* sick," joked Terry.

"I just heard on the news," said Skey. "A kid at my school got beat up." She rolled over to face the wall. "I wonder who it was."

Setting the tea on Skey's desk, Terry began to pull up a chair.

"I'm too tired, Terry," Skey said immediately. "I feel sick."

Terry hesitated, then put back the chair. "Get some sleep if you can," she said. "Don't forget to drink your tea."

"Did you put honey in it?" asked Skey, her voice suddenly childlike and climbing into a lisp.

"Lots of honey," said Terry, her voice warmed by an obvious smile. "Now rest."

The door closed.

IMMEDIATELY, SHE KNEW the boy wasn't here. In the long endless dark, there was no sense of him. She tried scanning with her mind, seeking with her instincts, but she couldn't locate him anywhere. For a long while she sat in the vast echoing solitude that surrounded her, holding the rock. Then she tried feeling her way along the carvings, touching their stories and whispering them to herself, but it wasn't her own story she needed to hear now, it was the boy's. Finally she realized where he must have gone. To date, she had never gone there by choice, and she knew he wasn't there by choice now. Taking a deep breath, she sought out the high white whine in her head, sent her thoughts into it and focused.

He was here. As soon as she arrived in the tunnel of light, she could feel the boy crouched somewhere, trapped in terror so fast, white and all-encompassing, it was like being plugged into an electrical socket. Huddled against a tunnel wall, she tried to scan for him, but it was impossible to penetrate the hostile brilliance. The light here hissed and screamed the way her mind did; there was no difference. This light *was* her mind, this system of tunnels an endless map of her own fear, and she had to crawl through it, meter by meter, looking for him.

THE EIGHT PM news downgraded Lick's condition to stable but didn't release his name, saying only that the victim had regained consciousness. Anyone who knew anything about the beating was advised to contact police. Switching off her radio, Skey returned to her bed and sent her mind back into the tunnel of light. She had to keep searching for the boy, she knew he was in here somewhere, could feel him.

"Skey?" called a voice. From far away came a knock, and then her door opened.

"Don't turn on the light," Skey said quickly. Opening her eyes, she watched the dark room take shape around her, the open doorway like a wound of light.

"Your friend San is on the phone," said Terry, leaning into the room. "Do you want to talk to her?"

"Yes," said Skey. Scrambling out of bed too quickly, she had to hang onto her desk until the blood stopped rushing to her head. Then she pulled on a housecoat and walked blinking into the unit.

The girls' phone sat on a coffee table outside the office, the receiver off its cradle. "San?" said Skey, sitting down in the chair beside it.

On the other side of the office window, Terry hovered casually.

"Just a minute," said San, and passed the phone to someone else.

"Skey," a male voice said abruptly. Skey's throat tightened. It was Jigger. "You tell anyone?" he asked.

"No," she said.

"You keep it quiet, you hear?" he said.

"Yeah," she said.

"He's not that bad," said Jigger. "Just a few bruises. Teach him to fall for my girl, eh?"

Tiny white cracks were starting to open across her brain.

"What's the matter?" asked Jigger. "First time I call you in that place to tell you I love you, and all you can say is no and yeah?"

Taking a deep breath, Skey pushed out a laugh. "C'mon San, you know he's like that with all the girls. You can't take him seriously."

There was a pause as Jigger thought through her response. "Staff listening?" he finally asked.

"Yeah," she said.

"Okay, I'll pick you up tomorrow at 8:20," he said. "You keep looking for a way to get us a key."

"Yeah yeah," said Skey.

Hanging up the phone, she looked around. The unit was still mostly empty, with just a few articles of furniture. Plaster glowed oddly where the walls had been patched. Suddenly it came to her, how impenetrable the lockup had seemed these past five months. Thick walls. Locked doors. Wired-over windows. Approved phone lists. Now she knew it took one kick and the walls crumbled. With one phone call, Jigger's voice had kicked its way in, and there was no plastering over that hole. For months she had imagined opening the side entrance door to outside, it was night, Jigger was standing in the snow waiting, she pulled him in through the shadows to her room where they made love, night staff missing every endless touch, every whimpering cry. But this afternoon had ended that dream. There was no going back to it now.

The boy was alone, somewhere in the tunnel of light. Getting up from her chair, Skey returned to her bed and rose into the white terror of her mind.

IT WAS 9:25, CLOSE to lights out. Skey had come out of the tunnel of light to take a break and was sitting, both arms resting on her knees while she stared at the scars. Twisted and jagged, they were like hieroglyphs, an indecipherable language. Meaningless, but they meant her. Why had she done it? She couldn't remember making the actual decision

They had been at Jigger's cabin on the May long weekend. Jigger had permission to be there with his guy friends—

Trevor, Balfour and Pedro. His parents didn't know the girls had also come along. The girls' parents thought they were at each other's homes. It had been easy to fool them. Parents wanted to be fooled.

"Jigger's such a nice boy," her mother was always chanting, like a refrain.

That night the gang had been heavy into various chemicals, a variety of altered states. Music had been pounding in the living room, but it had seemed distant, as if coming from another time and place. She could remember walking down a hall and into the kitchen. She had been naked, but she didn't know why. Pausing for a moment, she had stood scanning the empty room, then walked to a nearby counter, picked up a half-empty bottle of gin and smashed it on the side of the sink. Without pausing, she had lifted the bottle's jagged edge and dug it into her left forearm.

As the memory faded, Skey continued to sit and stare at her arms. A heavy ringing filled her ears and her brain felt sluggish, as if she had gone deep into herself, so deep she could barely breathe. She could remember doing the act—slashing her arms with the bottle—but not the reason why.

Tap tap. On the other side of the wall, Ann was beginning their nightly conversation. *Tap. Tap tap tap.* All of a sudden, white rage surged through Skey. Swinging around, she pounded her fist against the wall. From the next room came a muffled gasp and the squeak of bedsprings as Ann sprang back.

Almost immediately, there was a knock on the door. "Skey?" called Terry.

Huddled on the bed, Skey was shaking. "Yeah yeah," she mumbled.

The door opened and Terry's eyes zeroed in. "You all right?" she asked, slightly breathless.

"Yeah," said Skey. Breathing deeply, she closed her eyes.

"What was the bang?" asked Terry.

Skey shrugged. "Sorry," she said. "There's no hole. I didn't leave a hole."

"You punched your wall?" asked Terry.

"Just once," said Skey.

"So what's bugging you?" asked Terry.

I can't remember. She almost said it, then caught herself. "The guy on the bus," she shrugged.

"You want a go at the punching bag?" asked Terry.

"No," said Skey. "I'll be fine."

Terry hesitated, then asked, "What color are you feeling?"

A hiss passed through Skey and she said, "White."

Terry's eyes widened.

"I'm going to sleep now," said Skey and crawled between the sheets.

"All right," said Terry. "But keep it down in here. If I hear any more, we'll have to move you to the Back Room."

"Yeah yeah," muttered Skey.

SHE CLOSED HER EYES and her brain lit up: white ceiling, white walls, white floor—hissing, screaming white. Somewhere in this labyrinth, she could hear the boy giving off restless moans, then a long string of swear words. He didn't seem to be moving and she thought she could feel him curled into a ball, trying to shut out the light.

But he couldn't shut it out, just as she couldn't—this light was coming from inside their minds. Shuffling forward, she

gripped the rock in one hand while she felt her way along
the carvings with the other. In this wall, they all seemed to
move like water or blood, flowing toward him.

SKEY STEPPED HESITANTLY into the cold outside air, not
listening as the door closed behind her. Overnight it had
snowed, and she left tracks as she crossed the parking lot,
weaving between parked cars and nodding to teachers and
administration staff who were coming in for the day.

"Yeah yeah," she said, brushing off their greetings. It was
three blocks from the gate to the bus stop. Two blocks until
she would see him tapping the steering wheel. A block and a
half until she would have to say good morning and smile.

"Skey," called a voice.

She turned to see Jigger's car parked on a side street,
Jigger standing beside it, holding the passenger door open.
He had parked in a different spot this morning, closer—
hiding and waiting, hunting prey. "C'mon," he called, "over
here," but she stood frozen, staring at the boy and the car,
both of them picture perfect in the morning sun.

Jigger's such a nice boy, her mother's voice said in her
head.

Shoes crunched the snow-covered sidewalk behind her,
and she whirled to see Balfour coming up on her right.
At the same moment, Trevor stepped out from a tree and
Pedro appeared from behind another parked car. Counting
heartbeats, Skey took a single step toward Jigger, then
another.

"What d'you think?" she asked carefully. "I need an
armed guard?"

Jigger's face was just as careful. "Today the Dragons
decided to pick you up," he said.

"I live in a lockup," said Skey. "I thought you guys were supposed to be a break."

Without a word, Balfour's hand pressed itself against the small of her back.

"Everybody in," said Jigger.

Trevor and Pedro slid into the back seat, Balfour followed her into the front and pressed in on her right. Then Jigger came in for a kiss on her left, bringing the usual scent of tobacco and aftershave, the usual soft lips.

"G'morning," he grinned.

IN HOMEROOM, the pornographer sketched listlessly. All over the classroom, eyes kept flicking toward Lick's empty desk and away again. Already, everyone knew.

The expected announcement came over the PA. "Yesterday afternoon," said Mr. Leonardo, the principal, "there was a vicious attack on one of our students, Elwin Serkowski, who is now listed in stable condition at the South Side Hospital. Anyone who knows *anything at all* about this attack is asked to come forward with information."

From across the aisle, the pornographer glanced at Skey.

"What are you looking at?" she snapped.

Without speaking, he held up a full-page sketch of Skey and Lick at their desks, clothes on, nothing obscene. A picture of two friends talking.

Skey's eyes filled with tears. "Can I have it?" she whispered.

He shook his head.

"You're really good," she said.

"Maybe," he said.

"What's your name?" she asked.

"Amid," he said.

"Hello, Amid," said Skey.

BALFOUR WAS WAITING outside her History class, just before
lunch. "C'mon," he said. "Forget the jacket, we're heading
out."

"Bals," she protested, "it's cold."

Pulling off his sweatshirt, he handed it to her. "Wear
this," he grinned.

"No thanks," she said grimly.

Everyone else had already piled into Jigger's car. It was
a full load—Rosie, Balfour, San, Trevor and Gillian in the
back, Pedro, Skey and Jigger up front. Before they headed
off for lunch, Jigger stopped to do ten minutes of business
at a street corner three blocks from school. Then they ate
take-out from an A&W, listening to tunes as Jigger fed Skey
what she was allowed to take in. From the backseat came
the usual banter, Trevor sticking his fries under the neck of
San's sweater and nibbling, Balfour with one of his hands
constantly under Rosie's shirt. Rosie cooed, the guys called
out comments to passersby, and San and Gillian giggled.
Once upon a time, in a life long ago, Skey remembered
laughing with the others. How long ago had that been?
Yesterday? Last week? Before, or after, the scars?

"Friday, we rule," roared Balfour, throwing back his
head. "Oh, I've been dreaming about that place, all those
girls in their skimpy lingerie, asleep in their beds."

"Can it, Bals," Jigger said sharply.

Skey felt it then—the moment everyone sucked in their
breath and held it. Glancing into the backseat, she caught
San's eyes sliding off her own, and Trevor looking quickly
away—as if she had caught them watching to see if she
understood.

"Open the cage and free the little birdies," Balfour sang
softly, eyeing her.

The hair rose on the back of her neck, but Skey tried to make it casual. "What d'you guys want to do in there?" she asked. "Murder us all in our beds?"

"Pleasure," muttered Balfour. Rosie rolled her eyes and giggled.

Gently Jigger pulled her around to face him. "Night Games," he said, stroking her neck. "You know us, come and go. No one'll know we've been there except you."

"So this isn't going to turn into one of Balfour's fantasies?" Skey asked slowly.

Jigger laughed shortly. "We want to see where you live," he said, "not get thrown in the slammer. You think *we* want to do time in a lockup?"

On the radio, a song ended and the twelve thirty news came on. "Elwin Serkowski," said the announcer, "the young man who survived a gang beating yesterday afternoon has regained consciousness, but he's not talking. Apparently, he isn't saying a word. Police are asking anyone with information…"

Leaning forward, Jigger turned off the radio, then pulled Skey back in against himself. "You're not gonna tell on us, are you, baby?" he whispered. "You're my baby doll, aren't you, Skey? You just wanna be loved by me, I know you do, baby. Just wait 'til after school, 'til I dump these Dragons and we can be alone."

Jigger's arms wrapped tighter, his voice a heavy weight in her ear. She had to find the boy, the boy was the only one who understood. A flicker of intense light pulsed across the top of Skey's brain. She moved into it, the tunnel of light opened around her, and she was in.

HE WAS DIRECTLY in front of her, muttering the usual string

of swear words. Not wanting to startle him, she waited. Everything here was already so full of fear.

"Do you remember me?" she finally asked.

Immediately the swearing broke off. "Who are you?" asked the boy.

"I'm the girl from the tunnel," she said.

"What tunnel?" said the boy.

"The tunnel of dark where we usually meet," she said. "This is a different tunnel. You came here once before, to save me. You touched my hand."

"Huh?" demanded the boy.

His voice was slightly different—lower—but it was him. Had he somehow forgotten the tunnel of dark? Maybe the beating had damaged his brain so he couldn't remember.

"I don't know how I fucking got here, or who the hell you are," said the boy. "It's too bright to see anything in here. I remember guys from my school dragging me somewhere. I think they were going to beat me up. Then it got dark, and then I was here. The light's everywhere, and it's making a high-pitched sound. It's driving me nuts."

She leaned forward, her breath tight. "What's your name?" she asked.

"Elwin," said the boy. "Most people call me Lick."

She almost lost it then, the white whine sharpening to a drill in her head.

"Who are you?" asked Lick.

"Names are secrets," she whispered.

"Thanks a lot," he said.

"I'm going to get you out of here," she said. "I've just got to figure out how. D'you remember who those guys were?"

"Yeah," he said softly.

"D'you remember why they beat you up?" she asked.

There was a pause, and then Lick said, "Yeah, I remember."

She did lose it then. Without warning, the tunnel of light slipped out of her grasp, and she opened her eyes to find Jigger's hands cupping her face, his blue eyes staring into hers.

"What's the matter with you today?" he asked, giving her head a small shake. "You're some kind of zombie."

Skey blinked. *Jigger*, she thought frantically. She was with Jigger now. And when she was with Jigger, it was important to keep him happy, so he wouldn't suspect the other places she went to in order to do her true living, that slow steady groping toward some kind of truth.

"Jig," she whispered, pulling him in and kissing him softly, as softly as love could be imagined. "Jig, I love you, make me love you, make me yours, you know I want to be yours the whole night through."

Chapter Thirteen

When Skey told Ms. Fleck that her part of Group D's data was stored on Lick's mother's laptop, the teacher agreed to delay their presentation for a week. She then sent the class to the library to work on their assignment. Grabbing a thick important book, Skey ditched the rest of the group and headed to a back corner, where she sat down and placed the open book on her lap. Then she curved her hand over the rock in her pocket and whispered, "How do I bring Lick back to the dark tunnel?"

But the rock didn't seem interested in giving straight answers. Instead, a sharp crinkle of electricity shot across the top of her brain, and she was surrounded by the tunnel of light.

"Lick?" she said.

"That you again?" he asked. He sounded exhausted.

"Yeah," she said. "I'm trying to think of a way to get you back to the other tunnel."

"What are these tunnels?" he demanded querulously. "Some kind of experiment by the city's engineering department?"

"Try some kind of experiment with the human mind," she said.

"You mean we're inside our heads?" asked Lick.

"Something like that," she said. "We thought our way here."

"So whoever you are," said Lick, "you're as crazy as me."

"Almost," she said. "I hate this tunnel. It's like frying your brain circuitry."

"Tell me about it," he muttered.

"There's another tunnel," she said. "A dark one. Let's try thinking our way there."

Reaching into her pocket, she took out the rock and held it out in front of herself, moving it back and forth until she felt it bump into something.

"That you?" she asked.

"Maybe," he said.

"Okay," she said. "Touch this rock. I've got hold of it too. I think it can help us get there."

"Get where?" he muttered, but she felt his fingers graze against hers, then pull back to his side of the rock.

"Good," she said. "Now, just listen." Taking a deep breath, she began. "Think of the dark," she said slowly, "where no one can see you. No one can see what you look like, how you hold yourself, the way you think on your face. Think of the dark, where you see with your feelings and your fingertips, where your mind slows down so it belongs to you, and you can leave the pain behind. Think of the dark, where you can't see what happened to you, and so you can forget it. And when you have to go back to your regular life, you won't remember what they did to you, you can still be friends, you don't have to think about it at all. Think of the dark…"

It was happening, she realized, glancing around herself. The light was dimming, the air growing quieter.

"…where there are no expectations," she continued. "No one knows you, you can be alone, just a bit of life like a worm crawling along the ground, feeling your way along. There aren't even names; you are no one. The darkness is the place to be nothing, where nothing has ever happened to you and nothing ever will."

The last hint of light disappeared, leaving them standing in the dark tunnel, the air about them cool and damp, empty of vicious vibes. Leaning against the wall, Skey felt a trickle of water run down her back. She took deep shuddering breaths, breathing the dark, listening to Lick breathe himself quiet beside her. Gently she pulled the rock out of his fingers and pocketed it.

"This is better," he said. "Is it another one of those mind experiments?"

"Like a dream," she said. "It's like we met in the same dream."

"I could think of better dreams to meet in," muttered Lick.

"I like this dream," she said.

"This is the place you come to forget," said Lick.

An odd fear blew through her. "No," she said quickly. "No, I don't."

"That's what you said while you were bringing us here," said Lick. "It's the place to forget."

"No," she said again, cutting him off quickly. "I haven't forgotten anything. *You* forgot something, and I found you here."

"I've never been here before," said Lick, his voice stunned.

"Yes, you were," she said, "but you wouldn't tell me your

name. You couldn't remember anything then—your family, or your school, or even the city you lived in."

Lick hesitated, then spoke very carefully, as if she had completely lost it. "If I was here before," he said, "why can't I remember it?"

"I don't know," she said. "You told me you came here in a dream, and then you forgot where you came from. That's how I'm different from you—I remember the other side of my life, where my body lives."

"Where your *body* lives?" demanded Lick.

"This is a mind place," she said. "A place our minds live."

"Weird," muttered Lick. "I think you've got me mixed up with someone else. My name is Lick. And I remember everything. *Everything.* Believe me, there's stuff I'd rather forget."

In the darkness she stood silently, caught within the jagged edges of her heart. All she wanted was for things to fit together smoothly. "I don't understand," she said slowly. "All I know is the boy in the tunnel is you."

"Well, you're right about one thing," said Lick. "I don't want to go back."

"We'll be friends here," she said with a quick happiness. "You'll never get hungry or thirsty. You'll never need to sleep. I'll tell you about the carvings, and we'll feel our way along the tunnels just like before."

"Let's get one thing straight," Lick said emphatically. "I've never been here before."

For the first time in his presence, she felt alone. "All right," she said slowly.

"And one more thing," he added. "Don't touch me. It's bad enough when you can see the buggers who want to clap your shoulder and shake your hand, but in the dark, I'd freak. I don't know what I'd do to you."

Warmth came back to her. "I don't like it either," she said. "I won't touch you ever."

"Promise?" he asked.

"Promise," she said happily.

THEY WERE LYING in the backseat, wrapped in a blanket, the radio crooning as they curved together. "Y'see, Skey, y'see what we're like?" whispered Jigger. "It's so good between us. I swear it's never been like this with anyone else."

It was true. Even with everything that had happened, he had touched her today, and she had opened for him, the wonder flowing between them the way it always did. It made her sick. She hated touching, the way it betrayed her, made her feel such love.

"I know what we need, baby," said Jigger. "I know how to keep us together. What the Dragons did to that loser, I did it to keep us together. We gotta stick together. Dragons love their own kind, Skey. They love forever."

"You didn't have to put him in the hospital," she muttered.

"I told you to stay away from him but you didn't," Jigger said gently. "I had to put some sense into your pretty little head. You don't think right sometimes, you know you don't."

"I didn't want to fuck him," said Skey. "What's the big deal with talking to him?"

"Something wasn't right, I could feel it. But now it is." Softly Jigger kissed her. "You got that key yet?"

"No, but I know how to get it." Skey didn't want to argue, just get back to her room, the tunnel and Lick. "Why d'you want to come in at night anyway?"

"No questions, baby," said Jigger, sitting up. "It's your way of proving loyalty to the Dragons. Especially after what you've done." He started fishing around for his clothes.

Fear sang in Skey's mouth. "You want to hurt a girl, don't you?" she said. Wrapping the blanket tightly around herself, she stared at him. Jigger paused, then pulled his shirt over his head.

"We won't hurt you," he said.

"Someone else?" she whispered. "That's why you want to come in? You want to get a strange girl and hurt her?"

"Nah, Skey," said Jigger. "Why would we want to do that?" Leaning down, he kissed her. "Just Night Games," he soothed. "The usual. Hey, it's four fifteen. Time to get dressed."

Night Games. Dragons hunting. What do they talk about when I'm not around? thought Skey, staring at him. How had the gang changed since last May? Something was different. She could feel it in their silences, the ways they laughed, as if they had a joke that didn't include her, a joke she wouldn't want to know about. The Dragons hunted differently now, flew farther, clawed deeper.

Eyes narrowed, Skey stared as Jigger pulled on his jeans, kept staring as he turned and stared back at her, his face suddenly unreal, a stranger's face. Someone she had never seen. Who was this guy? Who was he, really?

"Get up!" he yelled, and she scrambled to put on her clothes, then tucked herself obediently under his arm. Playing with her hair, he steered the car into traffic, and she opened her mouth, soft-lipped, for his kiss.

"You let me handle all the big bad stuff," he said, "and we'll be fine."

"I love you, Jig," she replied. For the first time, she said it with fear. "I'll love you forever," she whispered.

Three blocks from the lockup, he let her out, pulled a U-turn and drove off. As Skey began walking, a car that had been behind them pulled alongside, and the front passenger door opened. Terry leaned across the seat toward her.

"Want a ride?" she called.

Blanking her face, Skey got in. It was warmer in this car, the radio talking politics, ways to improve the world. Ahead of them, the black iron gate loomed.

"Friend of yours?" asked Terry.

Skey gave up the game with relief. "Boyfriend," she admitted. "We've been going out for almost a year. You can call my mother. She'll tell you he's a very nice boy."

"And what do you think?" asked Terry quietly.

"He's my boyfriend," shrugged Skey. "I'm biased."

"So that's why you never need bus tickets?" said Terry.

"I use them," said Skey.

"Skey, you never even asked for them yesterday or today," said Terry.

Skey flushed. "I always get back by four thirty," she said, turning to look out her window. "Just ask my mother. He's a very nice boy."

As SKEY WALKED into the unit, a door slammed, then opened again, and she saw Ann come halfway out of her room. Body rigid, Ann stood staring at the unit. Both wrists were bandaged, she had obviously been scratching again. Standing beside the office, Skey hesitated, then started toward her own room. Immediately Ann's dark eyes fixed on her, and with a flash of guilt, Skey remembered how she had punched their shared wall last night.

Without a word, Ann backed into her room and slammed her door again. Quickly, Terry walked across the unit, knocked on her door and unlocked it. Voices poured through the open doorway, Ann yelling, Terry talking her down. Ann was going on about something stupid; everyone knew it wasn't what was really bothering her, but she kept yelling and Terry kept soothing. Eventually staff would calm Ann down, and the unit would get on with the usual.

Several feet from the office, Skey stood motionless. In the moment Ann's eyes had fixed on her, she had felt something pass from the other girl to herself, something cold and clammy, beyond words. Going into her room, she closed the door and sat on the bed, listening to the ebb and flow of voices on the other side of the wall. Slowly but surely, Ann was sinking into the calm of Terry's voice.

Ann, Skey thought suddenly, her heart leaping into her throat. What if the Dragons went after Ann? What would Balfour do to her? What would the Dragons do to any of the girls in this lockup—girls nobody wanted, girls locked away, forgotten. Losers.

But what would the Dragons do to her if she told? Or if she refused to let them in? She would be punished, and Jigger would almost certainly dump her. Since the first time they had made love, all she had wanted was more of the feelings that came with him, but he had never asked for something like this. How could she let the Dragons into a place full of sleeping girls? Girls with scratched wrists, slashed wrists. Girls tattooed with the names of all the boys who had never loved them.

When Terry left Ann's room, Skey moved over to the wall and started tapping on it. *Tap tap. Tap tap tap?* In the next room, Ann stopped pacing for a few seconds, then started again. With the exception of her attempt yesterday, it had been over a week since the two of them had done any tapping. Lifetimes came and went in a week.

On the other side of the wall Ann continued to pace, and Skey let it go. She had her own pain to search out. With a sigh of relief, she lay down on her bed and slid her hand around the rock in her pocket. Then she sent her mind into the dark.

THEY TALKED FOR hours. From what she could gather, Lick wasn't able to remember anything that had gone on between them in the dark, so she explained the layout of the tunnel system, the meeting places and the possibility of pits. Then she told him about the carvings, how she could feel them and he could not. Finally she began to tell him the stories she felt at her fingertips, the stories of her life. He listened as he had before, remembering what she said. What she didn't say.

She found one that twisted in agony, its nicks and bumps so sharp, she almost cut her fingertips. Barbed wire. "This is the way my mother screams," she told Lick. "This is the shape of her screaming."

"Why is she screaming?" he asked.

"She never said." Pressing gently, she ran a finger over the carving again. Her skin snagged, almost tearing open. Almost. *Almost.*

"Does she scream a lot?" asked Lick.

"Not anymore," she said. "My mother barely makes a sound."

"What did you do when she was screaming?" asked Lick.

"I hid," she said.

"Was she screaming at you?" asked Lick.

"No," she said.

They breathed a long pause.

"Where was your dad?" Lick asked finally.

"With her," she said.

Lick held the silence carefully. "Is that why you don't like to be touched?" he asked.

She hesitated. "Touching is a lie," she said slowly. "It hurts like it hurt my mother." She paused again. "It makes you feel good when it's the dragon's claw." Another pause came, and she whispered into it. "I don't know when it's true. I can't feel what's true in it."

"Feelings are tough," Lick whispered back.

"Feelings are shit," she said. "I want to get rid of them."

"Is that why your mother stopped screaming?" he asked. "She got rid of her feelings?"

She saw her mother in front of the TV, face empty and pale, flickering with the images on the screen. "Yes," she said.

They sat for a long time without moving, watching the dark.

Chapter Fourteen

There was a knock on her door. Mumbling irritably, Skey opened her eyes. Her clock radio read eight fourteen. "Yeah yeah," she sighed.

"Can you open up?" asked Terry.

Skey switched on the light, blinked rapidly for a few seconds and opened the door.

"Someone is here to see you," said Terry.

Alarm flashed through Skey. "Who?" she asked, her eyes skittering nervously.

"Come with me and see," said Terry, starting across the unit. Heart thudding, Skey followed her along the entrance hall and down the stairs.

"Where are we going?" she asked.

"In here," said Terry, turning into the first floor visitor's lounge. Then she sat down, leaving Skey standing in the doorway and facing two police officers: a woman and a man.

"Skey Mitchell?" asked the man.

Frozen to the spot, Skey stood staring.

"Perhaps you'd like to sit down," said the woman.

Without a word, Skey sat.

"We're here to ask you about the attack on Elwin Serkowski," said the woman. "Perhaps you've heard about it."

Skey's mouth twisted like thin metal wire. She nodded.

"Some students thought you might know something about it," said the woman, leaning forward in her chair. "Elwin seems to have lost all memory of the event. Temporary amnesia."

Skey found a spot on the wall and focused on it, letting the rest of the room fade into a blur.

"We're not suggesting you had anything to do with it," said the woman. "But if you have any knowledge of who was responsible, we'd like your help."

The high white whine in Skey's head was growing louder. Cracks opened across her brain, brightness oozed everywhere. Putting out a hand, she groped for a wall. Had she gotten caught in a meeting place? Was she standing at the edge of a pit? Was she already falling and she didn't even know?

"Skey," she heard someone say from a long ways off. Over and over, a voice kept repeating her name. "Skey," it said again. "Can you hear me? It's Terry."

The room came back into focus, and Skey found herself bent forward, both arms wrapped tightly around her waist. Tired, she was so tired. Slumping forward, she rested her head on her knees.

"It's all right, Skey, everything's okay," said Terry in a soothing voice. "Everything's just fine. How about we go back to the unit now?"

With a nod Skey straightened and saw that the police were gone. When had they left? Numbly, she followed Terry upstairs and into her room.

"I think we're going to give you a break from school tomorrow," said Terry.

Again, alarm jerked through Skey. "No," she said quickly, "I can't. I have to do a group presentation in English. It's on Shakespeare. I have to be there."

"I'm not sure you can handle it," Terry said dubiously.

"I can," said Skey. What would the Dragons do if she didn't show? What would they start planning? She had to be there to keep them sane.

"Skey," said Terry. "You had some difficulty speaking with the police."

"I can handle school," Skey said quickly. "I go to all my classes. I'm doing everything I'm supposed to. Call Ms. Renfrew tomorrow at the Counseling Department at lunchtime and ask her to check on me. I meet my tutor there on Wednesdays. I can even call you and check in if you want."

"Is your boyfriend picking you up before school?" asked Terry.

Skey's gaze flickered, but she forced it back to Terry's face.

"We've already contacted your mother," said Terry. "She gave us Alan's number and we called him. He's on your approved list now."

"Oh," said Skey. Sometimes she forgot Jigger's real name. "Great," she added brightly.

"So he can pick you up outside the door instead of waiting at the bus stop," said Terry.

Skey nodded and looked away.

"Skey," asked Terry, touching her arm. "Are you all right?"

"Yeah," said Skey, forcing her gaze back to Terry's a

second time. "Look, you've got lots of people you can check with to see how I'm doing. I'll be okay at school tomorrow, you'll see."

Terry nodded slowly, then said, "We'll call the Counseling office at lunch and check in with you."

"Okay," said Skey, tossing off another bright smile.

Still, Terry hesitated in the doorway. "Skey," she said finally, "do you know anything about the attack on Elwin Serkowski?"

White fire swept through Skey. "No," she said, her voice unexpectedly harsh.

Terry stretched time to its breaking point, then nodded and closed the door.

"WHAT ABOUT YOU?" she asked. "What are the stories of your life?"

"Nothing like yours," said Lick. "Just me and Mom, a house and a dog."

"What are you afraid of?" she asked. "Why don't you want to go back?"

"Why don't you?" he countered. "There's some reason you come here. Something you want to get away from."

"I already told you about that," she said quickly. "My mom. The screaming."

"It's something you've forgotten," persisted Lick. "You said this was a place for safety and forgetting."

"No, I didn't," she said, fighting off a surge of fear.

"Yes, you did," said Lick. "*Think of the dark where you can't see what happened to you and so you can forget it.* Those were your exact words."

Fear surged again, then twisted into anger. "Stop it," she screamed suddenly. "Just shut up about it, would you?"

Silence swelled between them, then shrank, leaving only the sound of their breathing.

"What I forgot is none of your business," she said finally. "It's nobody's business but mine."

"All right," he said. "Just so long as we both know it's there."

"Yeah, so it's there," she said irritably. "So what?"

"So you've got something, and I've got something," said Lick. "Except I know what mine is, and you don't remember."

"So why won't you tell me what yours is, then?" she asked.

"Because it's mine," he said simply.

THE FOLLOWING MORNING, Skey watched the side entrance door swing open onto a view of Jigger standing twenty feet away and holding open the passenger door to his car. Stepping into the brisk November wind, she slid into the front seat. Then she turned and waved to the staff watching through the wired-over window as Jigger closed her door and got in on his side.

"So, I'm approved?" he grinned, coming in for a short kiss, then pulling back—the staff was still watching. The car started up, the black gate loomed, and then they were through it and driving down the street.

"I can't believe I passed inspection," said Jigger. He howled once, a lone wolf sound, then asked, "You got that key?"

"Yeah," said Skey, blanking her face. Lying was easier than saying no.

"So hand it over," said Jigger.

"It's in my room," she said.

"What for?" he demanded.

"In case they frisk me," she said. "They did last Friday, remember?"

"Oh yeah," he said, staring off moodily. "How'd you get the key?"

"A volunteer," said Skey. "She must have holes in her pockets. She left it in one of the chairs she was sitting in."

The lockup had volunteers, but they certainly weren't given keys to the outside entrances. *Jigger wouldn't know that though*, thought Skey, sliding him a sideways glance. Fortunately for her, he knew very little about life on the inside.

"You're sure there's no alarm on that door?" he asked.

"Yeah," Skey said confidently. "It isn't a jail, y'know. It's a place for girls who are having problems. We're not criminals."

Jigger snorted. "Bunch of whores," he said, and Skey flinched. "Not you, baby," he added immediately. "I know you're different. You're just putting in time and then you'll be free. You'll be forever free." Steering with one hand, he slid an arm around her shoulders and started playing with her hair. "Free as the moon and the stars," he said softly.

She felt that distant from him, that far away.

"But for now," he said, stroking her cheek, "you're mine. All mine."

ONE MINUTE BEFORE the end of homeroom period, Lick walked through the door and stood in a back corner, staring as if he had never seen the place before. Rising from her seat, Skey was about to call out to him, but he turned and walked to the opposite side of the room, where he took a seat. Sinking back down, she watched him. Everyone in the

room watched him. Oblivious, Lick sat looking straight
ahead, without a shift or fidget, not a single loony spider
crawling up his legs. His left eye was purple-black, his nose
red and swollen, and his lower lip cut. A scrape ran the left
side of his face.

"Elwin?" said Mr. Pettifer, getting to his feet.

The bell rang, signaling the end of homeroom. Rising
with the others, Lick headed for the door.

"Elwin," Mr. Pettifer called again, but Lick exited the
room in a rush of thirty students. Right behind him, Skey
kept pace. She could see bruises on the back of his neck. All
she wanted was to reach out and touch him, touch some
part of him, find out who this was, who he could possibly
be.

"Lick?" called a guy, but the boy in front of Skey continued
on, not responding. A girl stopped in front of him, asking
how he was, and he stepped around her as if she was a tree
growing out of the floor—something in his way, that was
all. The crowd began to thin as students disappeared into
classrooms, and the halls cleared. As soon as possible, Lick
moved to the nearest wall and began to feel his way along
the lockers. Closing his eyes, he whispered a long string of
swear words.

It was the boy from the tunnel, the dark tunnel—the
boy she knew. But he didn't know her, he wouldn't recog-
nize Skey Mitchell by sight. And he didn't know anything
about this place, this school, this world—he had forgotten it
all when he dreamed his way into the tunnel and left Lick's
life behind.

The halls were now empty. Quietly, Skey moved to the
opposite wall. "Boy," she called softly. "Boy, it's me. Do you
remember me?"

Eyes still closed, he turned toward her, a look of recognition on his face. "You're here," he said gladly. "You're the girl with the stories in the wall."

"Yes," Skey said eagerly. "I'm here. Right here with you."

"I don't know where I am," he said, keeping his eyes closed. "I think I'm in a different dream now. I don't like this one. Too many people. How did you get here?"

"I come and go, remember?" said Skey. "I dream a lot of different dreams."

"You wearing your pj's in this dream?" asked the boy.

"Down, boy," grinned Skey.

"Just asking," he grinned back, without opening his eyes.

"Listen," she said softly. "Listen, and I'll tell you some more stories."

What could she tell him about this place? How could she help him understand his own life, the way it was now? Slowly they began moving along opposite walls, feeling their way.

"Did you find a carving yet?" he asked.

Abruptly, from behind them, came the sound of footsteps. "Elwin," called a woman.

Ducking into a nearby stairwell, Skey peered around the doorframe. Two figures were coming down the hall—Mr. Pettifer and a tall, thin, red-haired woman.

"Elwin, you're supposed to be at home, resting," the woman scolded gently, taking Lick's arm. "Why did you come to school when the doctor told you to stay in bed?"

The boy opened his eyes and looked around himself with a bewildered expression. "I found her," he said, "but now she's gone again."

"Who's gone?" asked the woman.

"The girl with the carvings in the wall," said the boy.

Frowning slightly, the woman glanced at Mr. Pettifer. "Let's go home, Elwin," she said softly.

"She's only here when it's dark," said the boy.

"You're okay now, Elwin," said Mr. Pettifer, taking his other arm. "Everything's okay."

"Don't touch me," said the boy, but neither adult let go of him.

Slowly they led him down the hall.

IN CALCULUS, San started imitating every move Skey made. When Skey put her chin in her hand, so did San. When Skey picked up her pen, so did San.

"Stop it," Skey hissed.

"Stop it," San hissed back.

It was such a little kid's game, but it gave Skey the creeps. The Dragons were closing in on her now, pulling her in so deep, she no longer owned her own movements.

CHAPTER FIFTEEN

WHEN SKEY WALKED INTO the Counseling office and saw Tammy sitting at their regular table, she felt as if the very atoms in the air opened to give her more space.

"Hungry?" asked Tammy.

"You bet," said Skey. "What've you got?"

"What you need," said Tammy. "More of these." With a smile, she slid two meat pastries across the table. Grabbing one, Skey chomped her way through it, then downed the orange juice Tammy handed her.

"When I get out of that lockup," she said, letting out a small burp. "I am going to take you out for a fabulous lunch."

"Oh yeah?" said Tammy. "Where?"

"Anywhere you want," said Skey. "We can go to the Bean Palace Extraordinaire if you want. You can bring your mother too. I owe her." Eagerly she began munching the second pastry.

"You don't owe," said Tammy dramatically, leaning toward her. "You deserve."

Skey's throat tightened, and she set down the pastry. "You have no idea," she whispered, staring at the table.

"About what?" asked Tammy.

"You're another world," Skey said slowly.

"No," said Tammy. "We're the same world, you and me."

Skey shook her head. "Different planets," she said.

"Look around you, girl," said Tammy. "Do you see me on a different planet from you?"

Hesitantly, Skey met the other girl's eyes. "Then how did you get to be so different?" she asked.

"My mother *feeds* me," Tammy said emphatically.

"That's not all it is," said Skey, toying with the pastry. "You ever had…sex, Tammy?"

Tammy's eyes widened. "No," she said, glancing away.

"Why not?" asked Skey.

Tammy flushed. "I'm not exactly on the Most Wanted List, am I?" she said.

"You could get it if you wanted," said Skey.

Tammy let out a nervous whoosh of air, then said, "Why are we talking about this?"

Skey focused on a spot just to the left of Tammy's face. "Sex changes things," she said quietly. "When a guy wants you, when *guys* want you, you don't belong to yourself anymore. You belong to them, to their eyes and their hands. To their thoughts. They've got you, trapped in their minds, doing whatever they want you to do." She paused, thinking. "It starts in grade six or seven, as soon as they figure out what their cocks are for. That's when they start watching, trapping you with their minds. And their mouths. No matter what they're saying, what they're telling you is, *You're mine. If you don't get it from me, you'll get it from some other guy. Then you'll belong to him.*"

"So don't listen to them," said Tammy.

"They're not *asking* you to listen," Skey said intensely. "They're not *asking* for anything. If they were *asking*, you could *answer* no."

Tammy's gaze faltered, and she took a deep breath. "I'm not sure," she said slowly, "what we're talking about."

"How do I get myself back?" Skey asked softly. "What I want to know is how do I take myself back—back from the dragon's claw?"

Across the table, the two girls watched each other silently.

"How well do you know this dragon?" asked Tammy.

"Pretty well," said Skey.

"How well do you know yourself?" asked Tammy.

Skey's eyes dropped.

"I don't know about dragons," said Tammy, "but yourself you can do something about."

Skey stared at the long sleeves covering her forearms. "Maybe," she said.

AT THE END OF the tutoring session, Skey borrowed enough money for bus fare from Tammy and caught the bus back to the lockup. Tammy was right, she thought, watching through the window as the city slid past. It didn't matter how well she knew Jigger and the Dragons, and it didn't matter if she guessed their intentions and realized what they planned to do. She didn't own them, she didn't run that pack, and she couldn't change a single electrical pulse in their brains. What she needed most right now was to go deeper into herself. That was where the possibilities lay, the search for what she could become.

"I feel sick," she told Janey upon her return to the unit and crawled into bed. Then she closed her eyes and descended into the relief of her mind. "You're right," she said quietly into the dark. "There is something I need to remember, but I don't know how. How do I remember something when I don't know what it is?"

"What are you most afraid of?" asked Lick.

"Touch," she said immediately. But it was more than that, and she knew it. And if she couldn't say it here in the dark to someone who would never know who she was, how could she truly face it within herself?

"Turning on," she added shakily. "Turning on to the dragon's claw. Wanting it."

"Wanting what makes you scream?" asked Lick.

She saw what he was getting at. "Wanting what made my mother scream?" she asked.

"Yeah," he said.

"Everyone's got their own personal dragon," she said. "I'm pretty sure my mother made herself forget she ever had one."

"I never forgot mine," said Lick. "I can't forget. I *want* to. You're lucky. Why d'you want to remember what makes you afraid?"

"I feel like I'm missing part of myself," she said. "Like an arm or a leg. Or maybe part of my brain—the part that helps me think straight."

Lick laughed softly. "So you can think like me?" he asked. "So you can think about it all the time, always scared, always thinking he's coming to get you again, it's going to happen again, it's going to happen any minute and you can't stop it, you're helpless, you're an *absolute victim*. You want to remember how bad it got, how much you *begged* for him to stop, how you screamed? How you wanted it to end, how you just wanted everything to end?"

"I tried to kill myself," she said.

Lick continued shakily. "I remember knowing it would never end," he said. "I remember my face pushed into my pillow, so no one could hear me screaming. I remember him bringing in his buddies, and it'd be a group thing. Sticks and bottles, not just body parts. I remember telling my mother, and her not believing me. For twelve years, she didn't believe me. Asked him to *babysit* me. Finally, she walked in and saw it happening. Then she believed me. She ran straight to the phone and called the cops. I was fourteen years old, but she held me in her lap and rocked and rocked me until they came. Rocked and rocked me while I answered their questions. She wouldn't let go of me. I hated her touching me, I hated anyone touching me, but she wouldn't let go."

"Did he go to jail?" she whispered. "Your dad?"

"Not my dad," said Lick. "He was gone a long time ago. It was my brother. He's seven years older than me. The judge gave him two years less a day. I think he did six months, and then he was out on good behavior."

She let out a long string of swear words.

"You got it," Lick said softly. "Oh, I remember. I remember *everything*. Sometimes I get these sharp stabbing pains in my ass, like someone's got a shovel and he's digging me wide open. Then I know my brother is thinking about me. I know he's thinking about me. I know he's thinking about me."

Lick whimpered softly, drowning in his memories, his fear. *Her fear.* She felt it like Lick felt it, but still she knew something he didn't. Part of him *had* forgotten, just as she had. The boy in the tunnel was his forgetting. The boy with the secret name, the boy with no name—Lick didn't know about that part of himself. That meant he only had one side of the story, one side of himself, just like she had. And now she had to figure out how to find the other side of herself.

"I've got to know," she whispered. "I've got to."

"It's your funeral," said Lick.

OUT IN THE UNIT, Ann was obviously having another bad day, stalking around, yelling at staff, and slamming her door. Finally, just before evening snack time, staff moved her to the Back Room to cool off, and quiet descended onto Skey's room. Settling onto her bed, she took one last look at the stars and prepared to descend again into the dark tunnel.

"Skey," called a staff. "Phone."

Heart thudding, Skey picked up the girls' phone to find Jigger on the other end of the line. "What do you think you're pulling?" he demanded, his breath heavy and harsh.

"What d'you mean?' she stammered.

"Where were you this afternoon?" he asked.

"I got sick," she said. "I came home."

"That isn't *home*," he hissed. "It's a dungeon, remember?"

Surprise flickered through Skey. She had actually called this place home. "Yeah, okay," she mumbled.

"Plans have changed," he said abruptly. "You'll be required to prove your loyalty to the Dragons tonight. Two AM. You've got the key. Meet us at the door and let us in."

"No, Jig—," she started to protest, but Jigger cut her off.

"Night Games," he said and hung up.

SKEY LAY WATCHING the red numbers on her clock radio flick past midnight, closing her eyes tightly each time night staff came around with a flashlight, checking the rooms. After Jigger's phone call, she had crawled into bed and glued her eyes to the clock. Whatever Lick was thinking about in the dark tunnel, tonight he would have to think about it alone—she had to make sure she was here and awake for two AM, so she could show the Dragons that she had no key. Then they would go away, and it would be over. There would be no Night Games in this place of girls, no Night Games for Ann or anyone else who was alone, hurt and scared.

HER CLOCK READ 1:15. Skey figured she would give herself time to get down the stairs, but not so much that staff would see her hanging around the side entrance door. As far as she could tell, the girls' rooms were checked once an hour—at ten thirty, eleven thirty and twelve thirty. The next time would be one thirty. No, a little earlier. At exactly one twenty-four, a brilliant flashlight beam swept over her closed eyelids and passed on.

Skey sat up slowly, cringing at the creak of bedsprings. She waited, hunched over her thudding heart, but the flashlight didn't return. Getting out of bed, she peered through her open doorway, watching the night staff move around the unit, tidying up. At one forty, the woman turned on the TV, then sat down and lit a cigarette, breaking the no-smoking rule.

Move, Skey thought, clenching and unclenching her hands. *You've got to move.*

The minutes crawled by, and she began to go stiff at the knees. Finally, at one fifty-two, the woman stood and went into the girls' washroom. Immediately Skey ran past the office and down the entrance hall. Here she paused at the edge of the brightly lit main hallway, where the stairs began their descent.

She knew how each one of the stairs creaked. One wrong

move, and sound would reverberate through the entire building. How could Jigger think the Dragons would be able to sneak into this place? Coming up these stairs, they would broadcast themselves in stereo. Carefully, Skey began her odyssey down the stairwell, sliding from one end of a stair to the next. Meticulously, she picked her way through a minefield of hidden noise and gradually gained the first landing, then the second and finally the last eight steps that led toward the side entrance door.

She approached the door slowly, knowing they were already there, feeling them shift in the outside dark. She could feel them and they could see her through the window, well-lit in the hall light. As she neared the door, cold air blew in under the bottom and onto her bare feet. Now she could see dark shapes and pale faces. Somehow the gang had turned off the outside light above the door—unscrewed it, probably. Abruptly, Balfour's leering face squished itself against the window, his eyes rolling, his mouth large and distorted. Behind him, San drifted close enough to be seen, then faded back. Stepping forward, Jigger motioned for her to unlock the door.

Open the door, he mouthed in huge syllables as if she was stupid. *Open the door.*

In slow motion, Skey spread her hands and pressed her empty palms against the window glass. *No key*, she thought at them urgently. *I have no key.*

"Shit," Jigger said quietly, but the gang didn't fade away into the night. Instead, Jigger gestured to Trevor, who hunched down over the outside keyhole. Pressing her face to the glass, Skey heard a slight scraping sound, and realized what he was doing. Trevor was using a pick. The Dragons were trying to pick the lock.

She understood then. They hadn't come to play the usual Night Games. They hadn't even come to get at a feast of sleeping girls, torture and mutilate them in their beds. They had come hunting for her. She had betrayed them, turned on her own kind, and they could feel it—they were the same blood and heartbeat, weren't they? The Dragons were going to pick the lock, open the door, pull her out into the night, and take her away.

Forever free, she remembered Jigger saying, sad and soft. *Free as the moon and the stars.* Whatever he planned to do with her, she wouldn't be coming back.

Electric fear surged through Skey, and her empty hands came together into fists. Desperately she began pounding on the door, the dark sound of her hands echoing beneath her high bright voice. No words, but enough sound—endless, terrified sound.

In the distance, she could hear night staff coming, calling out to her as they descended the stairs. With a moan, Skey slumped to the floor, her head filling with the sound of running feet, panting, the slam of a car door and an engine starting up. On the other side of the locked door, wheels spun and squealed down the street, taking seven Dragons away from what might have been, what they would have done to her, the fate the dragon's claw had reserved for each one of them that night.

Chapter Sixteen

Skey woke in a tiny room with a single bed and a small wire-crossed window. Daylight poured through the glass. As she rolled over to look at it, exhaustion lapped at her body like an inner ocean. Through the wall beside the bed, she could hear muffled voices—staff joking with Monica, who had come to the office to ask for a tampon. So, thought Skey, looking around herself, she had finally made it into the Back Room, where they kept the crazy girls. Skey Mitchell had finally lost it so bad, they didn't even trust her in her own bed.

Every fifteen minutes, staff checked in on her. When they saw that she was awake, they brought her some clothing and she got dressed. Mid-morning, Larry came to see her. He brought a gray-cushioned chair with him, nothing his weird fashion sense could argue with. Mrs. Mitchell would have been pleased.

"I hear you took a walk last night," he said, sitting down. "You want to tell me about it?"

Seated on the bed, Skey closed her eyes and worked her way through the possibilities. Staff must suspect that she had been waiting for someone at the side entrance, but they wouldn't have any proof. The Dragons probably hadn't left any noticeable tracks last night—it hadn't snowed recently, and a zillion people walked in and out of that door every day.

"I was sleepwalking," she said, flashing Larry a glance. "I had a nightmare."

Larry gazed back at her as if he had time on hold. "Do you remember your nightmare?" he asked finally.

The first thought that came to her was the tunnel of light. "I was in a hallway where it was too bright," she said quickly. "I couldn't see anything, because my head was filled with this burning light. I was trying to get out."

She thought it sounded like the right kind of nightmare, but Larry's eyes weren't buying it. "You timed it well," he commented. "Not a single night staff spotted you. How did you get down all those creaky steps without a sound?"

"I dunno," said Skey. "I was sleepwalking, remember?"

Larry leaned forward, his eyes intent. "Skey," he said, "something terrible happened to you last night. You were very frightened when staff found you. Screaming. You wouldn't let anyone touch you. We can help you if you let us know what's going on."

The faces of seven Dragons appeared in Skey's mind, lit up and hissing like the tunnel of light. "I feel sick," she mumbled, hugging herself. "I think I might throw up."

Larry backed off immediately. "Okay," he said, picking up his chair. "I'll let you rest now and come back later."

After he left, Skey sat on the bed, staring at a line of trees outside the window. In the late morning wind, they were bending and swaying, rowing into the wind and the sky. *Keep going, keep going,* she thought, the words heavy and old in her head. Staff continued to check her at fifteen-minute intervals. At noon, she heard the girls return to the unit for lunch, then leave again for school. The afternoon shift came on. Muffled scraps of conversation leaked through the wall, something about Ann and her birthday tomorrow.

"…probably the reason for her acting out," said someone, and Skey stiffened. What did staff think was the reason for Skey Mitchell's "acting out"?

She had left the rock in her jeans, which were hanging in her room. It was no longer necessary for her to be touching it before connecting with the dark tunnel, but all she could seem to manage was sitting on this bed, staring out at the empty swaying trees, while she kept her heart beating and her lungs taking in air. It was so much work just to stare.

AFTER SUPPER, staff moved her back to her own room. Every half hour or so, one of them would knock on the door, poke in a head, and try for a bit of chitchat. Seated on her bed, Skey simply stared out the window. Over the past hour, the sky had grown noticeably darker and the trees quieter. The stars were beginning to show. *As free as the moon and the stars,* she remembered, watching them. What Jigger had meant, she now realized, was dead, her soul gone out to sing with the stars. Well, even without the Dragons's help, her soul was out there singing with the stars, because she was empty, a blank staring shell. The Dragons were gone, and so was she.

She left the rock in her jeans, hanging in the closet.

On the other side of her door, the unit was unusually quiet. There had been a party for Ann, with a few girls from Units A and C attending, but they had left a half hour ago. Contrary to what staff had predicted, Ann seemed to be behaving for her fifteenth birthday—no yelling, no door slamming, no "acting out." Staff must be relieved.

OUTSIDE SKEY'S WINDOW, the sky grew darker, the stars brighter. Her soul shone farther and farther away. *I'm with my mother now,* she thought dully. *Nothing and no one can reach us.*

Through the wall, she heard Ann go into her room and close the door. Then it was quiet, not even the squeak of bedsprings, as if the birthday girl was standing in the middle of that small narrow space, deciding what to do. How to do it. After a bit, Skey heard the muffled sound of a large object being pushed across the floor, slowly, so no one would hear. Only one thing in Ann's room was that large—the bed. She was pushing her bed across her door to block it.

Skey came alive as if her brain hadn't functioned for a long time. Thinking without words, without language or eyes. Instinctively, the lower, darker part of her brain began sniffing out the silence in Ann's room. In Ann. Without seeing, that part of Skey's brain understood the soft sound of a dresser drawer sliding open, and the subsequent silence as Ann's hand fumbled for something among her clothing. Something hidden. Something small with a sharp edge. She had it. The birthday girl had the tiny weapon in her hand, the weapon that would cut her open and call out the blood.

Ann was silent, but Skey was screaming. Grabbing the chair next to her desk, she dragged it onto her bed. She had learned from last night and the riot—the walls and doors of this place were illusions. With another scream, Skey swung the chair at the wall and saw it buckle slightly. She swung again, and a large hole appeared. Dropping the chair, she pulled aside a dangling piece of plaster, then dove through the hole and onto Ann's bed. Without pausing, she scrambled to her feet and lunged at the girl standing two feet away and holding a small piece of broken glass to her throat. The first small cut was already bleeding.

"No," sobbed Skey, wrapping her arms around Ann. "No, baby, put that ugly thing down. Don't do that, baby, you don't deserve that, baby."

With an answering sob, Ann began to shake, and the two of them sank together to the floor. Taking the glass from Ann's hand, Skey threw it across the room.

"No, no, no," they whispered brokenly to each other. *No, baby, don't do that, baby, you want your skin to live free.*

WHEN STAFF CAME crawling through the hole in the wall, Skey started screaming again. Mindless white-hot panic erupted in her, so heated, it blurred her vision and shut out external sound. On the other side of her fear, vague gray shapes tried to calm her, but she backed into a corner, trying to fend them off. Quickly Ann's bed was shoved aside, and two of the blurred shapes took hold of Skey's arms. Suddenly hands seemed to be everywhere, grabbing and pushing her toward the now open door. Trapped in the high bright terror of her mind, she bit and kicked, dimly aware that she was being taken down stairs, then carried along the long indoor passageway that led to the school. A door was unlocked, then another, and another. Abruptly, she was pushed into a small quiet space. The hands let go. She was released.

BUT THE SCREAMS wouldn't release her. Unabated, terror continued to pour its high bright light into Skey's mind.

Trying to get rid of it, to somehow reduce it to human size, she ran herself repeatedly against the padded walls of the room into which she had been placed. Even though staff had retreated and locked the door behind them, hands still seemed to be reaching out to grab her—invisible hands, hands that weren't really there, hands coming out of nowhere.

There is no one here, she thought, knowing that she was alone in a small locked room with staff monitoring her through a wire-crossed window in the door, but she continued to feel invisible hands grabbing her arms and pushing her down, and then a single hand, pressed over her mouth. Screaming and sobbing, Skey slid to the floor. Now she felt her legs being shoved apart and heard voices speaking—Jigger telling someone to be gentle, Trevor telling her to calm down and Balfour laughing. Then Pedro, saying something she couldn't make out.

Skey's vision began to clear, and she saw that she was descending through a thick white light. Then the thick light faded, and she found herself in the master bedroom at Jigger's cabin. Immediately she realized that she was back in the May long weekend, six months previous. Music pounded through the walls—everyone was partying in the living room, except her and Jigger. When the rest of the gang had started taking off their clothes, she had panicked, and he had brought her in here. Like he said, he always made an exception for her, he was so good to her, didn't make her do what the other girls had to do. She was special, his and his alone, and they were making love on the bed, it was so wonderful to have a bed instead of a backseat, the soft sheets encasing them, their bodies moving gently against each other.

The bedroom door opened, and Trevor, Pedro and Balfour walked in naked. "Jigger," Skey whispered, shrinking down under him, trying to cover herself. But instead of protecting her, Jigger did the unthinkable, lifted himself up and kicked off the sheets.

"This is your true initiation," he said, holding her down by the shoulders. "We're together in this gang. Everyone is one. This is the way you show you're part of the Dragons."

"No," Skey whispered, staring up at him. "No." But Jigger didn't listen. Turning to the others, he told them to be gentle, just hold her down, she was already wet and ready, they wouldn't have any problems getting in. Someone held Skey's arms, someone else pushed apart her legs. When she started to scream, a hand covered her mouth.

Jigger was right. They slid in easily, and then they moved slowly. It wasn't *wham bam, thank you ma'am*, it was worse. Each Dragon raped her as gently as true love, slow and easy, swearing ecstasy in her face. "You like it, baby, you like it, don't you?" they whispered, watching as her body responded, as her screams became different cries. "See, you like it, Skey," they said, grinning. "You like it, baby, you like it." Time after time, she came and they came. They rotated on her, took turns, kept going. After a while she stopped coming; a while after that, waves of nausea took her into blackout.

When she came to, she was alone. Someone had covered her with a sheet. Through the wall, she could hear the party still going in the next room. Her first movement sent a raw pain tearing through her groin. She whimpered and felt her throat burn. Bewildered, she looked around herself. What was she doing here? She couldn't remember. Where was Jigger? Was he…?

Vague memories swung through her head: Jigger, Balfour and Trevor, close and leering. Pedro, panting above her. *No, it couldn't be,* she thought, panicking. *It couldn't.*

Sitting up, she dragged her legs over the edge of the bed. Waves of pain seared her groin, then gradually began to fade, taking the memories with them. When Skey finally stood up, her body felt as pain-free and numb as rubber. Step by step, her pain-free rubber legs took pain-free rubber steps to the bedroom door. Opening it, she walked her pain-free rubber walk down the hall and into the kitchen, ignoring the party to her left.

As soon as she entered the room, her eyes zeroed in on the bottle of gin on the counter. One quick smash, and she had all the sharp edges a girl could want. Stretching out a pain-free rubber arm, she jabbed at it, deep twisting jabs. Blood poured down her arm, and she felt nothing. Each jab pushed the pain farther away. Each gash sent the vague memories deeper, into a place where she would never find them, where they could be forgotten, where they had never happened, had never been real.

After she switched arms, someone came into the kitchen. Suddenly Dragons were everywhere, yelling and running as Skey stood silently in their midst, letting them wrap her arms, dress her in her clothes, put her in a car and drive her to a hospital, where her arms were sewn up. In the middle of all that medical equipment and expertise, no one thought to check for a wound between her legs. Skey didn't mention it. She had forgotten it. She had become the still quiet eye at the center of the storm.

SKEY HAD NEVER heard such silence. Lying on the floor of the small padded room, she let her arms splay outward and floated on absolute weariness. For the moment she felt oddly safe, as if something, some terrifying undefined *thing* that had lived deep within her, had finally been released. With that release came a kind of knowing, an understanding of where she would find her missing part. Returning in her mind to look at the cabin bedroom, Skey saw her lost part still lying on the bed. Above her head, close to the ceiling, was a glowing tunnel of light that traveled through the room, then on into the wall and what lay beyond it. Below the tunnel of light, at floor level, traveled a parallel dark tunnel—two alternate dimensions, one of bright mind-searing terror, the other of night-blind forgetting and safety.

So this was where she had first found the tunnels, thought Skey, staring at them—here in the cabin bedroom, during the rape or after, while she had lain alone, unconscious. The tunnels had been ways to escape, ways to forget what had been too difficult to remember. At the same time, they had become dimensions of searching for what had been lost. Losers were people who had lost something. The tunnels of darkness and light had always existed, they would always be there for the losers who needed them. The tunnels were dreams where losers could go.

In her mind, Skey reached out. Stepping into the memory of that cabin bedroom, she walked over to the bed and took the hands of the naked girl who lay there.

"I love you," she said quietly. "I've come to take you home."

The girl sat up. Slowly their arms slipped around one another, Skey and her lost part pulling each other close. Closer. Then, like the taking in of breath, the other girl slipped into Skey, and they were one.

"HOW ARE YOU feeling?" asked a voice. Looking up from her position on the floor, Skey saw Terry standing in the unlocked doorway.

"Terry?" she said, squinting at the staff. "Turn out the light, would you?"

"I need to be able to see you," said Terry.

"There's light from the hall," said Skey. "I can talk better in the dark."

Terry hesitated, then switched off the light. "Where would you like me to be?" she asked. "Would you be more comfortable if I stayed here in the doorway?"

"You can come in," said Skey.

Quietly Terry entered and sat down beside her. With a groan, Skey sat up and leaned against the wall. She was so tired. Dizziness lifted heavy wings in her head and flew off slowly.

"Terry," whispered Skey, her eyes closed. "I want to be somebody."

"You are," Terry whispered back.

"No," said Skey. "I'm a thing. A machine. When they did that to me, I didn't want it. I wanted Jigger, but I didn't want the rest. But it didn't matter. It was the dragon's claw, and I still turned on." Skey stumbled over her words, frightened at their hugeness. "I'm a thing," she repeated, her face twisting. "A *thing.*"

"Skey," Terry said slowly. "Are you talking about a rape?"

Skey nodded once.

"A gang rape?" asked Terry.

Skey's breathing snagged. She nodded again.

"And you had an orgasm?" asked Terry.

"Yes," Skey whispered.

188   BETH GOOBIE

Terry touched her arm. "That happens to many girls and women who are raped," she said gently. "It doesn't mean you wanted to be raped."

Within Skey, something opened—hope, the possibility of being human. "Then, why does it happen?" she asked, opening her eyes.

"Your body wants to give life," said Terry. "That's why it gives you orgasms. The body wants to make sex pleasurable so you'll conceive a child, but it doesn't always know the difference between making love and rape. It just wants to make sure you keep going until you've conceived, so it gives you pleasure."

"I was with my boyfriend first," said Skey. "Then the others came in."

"Makes even more sense," Terry said firmly. "You were probably in a state of arousal before it happened."

She's all wet and ready, Skey remembered, her mouth trembling. *You'll slide in easy.*

"Yes," she whispered. "I was."

"You weren't responding like a machine," said Terry. "You responded to your boyfriend. Then the others came in."

Behind Terry's back, the light from the doorway was fading, the room around them going dark. *Too much*, Skey thought wearily. She needed to retreat into the dark tunnel again and rest.

"Skey," called Terry, but already Skey could feel Lick's presence materializing beside her in the dark.

"Weird," he said. "I can see a blue-green glow when you first come in."

"First day of a bruise?" she asked.

"Morning on the ocean," he replied. "Beautiful."

In the distance, she could hear Terry call her name a second time. Putting out a hand, she touched the tunnel wall and found a long thin wave with sharp nicks.

"Skey," Terry called again.

"Can you hear her?" she asked, turning to Lick. "Can you hear her calling?"

"Hear who?" he asked.

"Terry," said Skey, turning back to the staff on her other side. "We're in the dark now. Can you feel it?"

"Wherever you are, I'm with you," said Terry.

"The carvings," said Skey. "I want you to feel the carvings." Reaching out, she fumbled for Terry's hand, then guided it along the carving, tracing the full length of the wave.

"Can you feel it?" she asked.

"Yes," said Terry.

"It's a scream," said Skey. "My own scream. It hurts."

Around her the darkness began to fade, taking Lick with it. In its place, the padded room and doorway of light reappeared, and she saw that she continued to sit beside Terry, between the dark and the light—enough light to see by, enough darkness to keep them safe. In her hand, she still held Terry's, and now she noticed that she was gently moving the woman's fingertips across one of the scars on her left forearm.

Carvings, Skey thought in astonishment. *Scars. Stories in the tunnel wall, stories in my skin.*

With a gasp, she dropped Terry's hand and ran her own fingertips across the scar, feeling it carefully, then shifted her fingertips to the other scars on her left forearm. Beneath her touch, they hurt with fresh pain, jagged and deep as if they had just been cut. Cradling her arms against her stomach, Skey began to rock.

"How's Ann?" she asked.

"Ann will be fine," said Terry.

"Sorry about the wall," said Skey. "My parents will pay for it."

"We'll work something out," said Terry.

"Will I go to the detention center?" asked Skey.

"No," Terry said firmly. "It wasn't a riot, Skey. Ann might have been dead, if it wasn't for you."

"I didn't want her to have any scars," said Skey. "I didn't know she was cutting her throat."

"She was," said Terry. "And you stopped her."

With a sigh, Skey crawled onto Terry's lap and burrowed her face in the woman's neck. "I stopped her," she whispered.

Terry's arms came around her, and they rocked.

CHAPTER SEVENTEEN

SIDE BY SIDE, Skey and Terry walked up the front steps of a small bungalow. From inside the door came a mad scrabbling of paws and a furious yapping. Seconds later the door opened, and they were greeted by a ferocious growling Corgi.

"Shh, Microbe," said Lick's mother, pushing back the dog with her foot.

"Microbe!" said Skey, staring at the animal.

"My son named him," Lick's mother said apologetically. She glanced at Skey and her eyes widened. "You're the girl in the hall," she said. "When I came to get him at school that day…"

"Yes," said Skey.

"And you think you can help him?" asked Lick's mother.

"I hope so," said Skey.

Stepping inside, she scanned the thin red-haired woman standing before her, the mother who hadn't believed her youngest son for twelve years, then had believed him absolutely. In spite of what Skey had recently told her own

mother, Mrs. Mitchell was still saying, "But Jigger's such a
nice boy. His father owns Full Circle Real Estate."

THE COURT HEARINGS were over, and the trial dates set.
Skey's statement about the two assaults—the physical one
against Lick and the sexual one against herself—had put the
four male Dragons into the youth detention center, where
they would remain until their trials. Lick still hadn't given
his statement, but that wasn't the primary reason Skey had
decided to visit him. No, the real reason she had come here
today was because she needed him. Here, in the real world,
where he belonged. Where both sides of himself belonged.

"He's still not talking," his mother said warningly. "Just
sits in his room, saying nothing."

"Can I go in?" asked Skey.

Ms. Serkowski nodded.

"Alone?" asked Skey.

Lick's mother glanced at Terry, who nodded. Leaving
them in the front hall, Skey walked down a short hall that
Ms. Serkowski had pointed out, then stopped at the first
open doorway. Glancing through it, she saw that the walls
were plastered with posters, but the room was deadly clean,
obviously taken care of by a mother. Lick hadn't been here
in a long time. Sitting on the bed, she could see the boy
from the tunnel, his eyes closed as he whispered to himself.
Quietly Skey stood in the doorway, listening. Yes, it was still
the same code—a long string of swear words, meticulously
phrased.

"I'm here," she said finally.

"It's you," said the boy. Smiling, he turned his face
toward her. The bruises and black eye had faded, and the
scrape scab on his left cheek was beginning to lift at the

edges. Eyes still closed, he turned his head, following her movements as she pulled up a chair and sat down.

"Yes," said Skey. "I'm the girl with the carvings."

"You've been gone a long time," he said.

"But I've come back," she said.

"I was trying to feel for your carvings," he said, frowning. "It got so quiet, I thought I'd make up some stories for myself. But I couldn't find any ideas in the walls. Nothing."

"They were just there for me," she said. "Only I could feel them."

"I'm in a weird dream now," he said. "I don't like it. I want to go back to the tunnel, but I don't know how."

"I think I have a solution," Skey said carefully.

"You do?" asked the boy. He straightened, and she watched the thoughts run across his face.

"Remember," she said, "how I always came and went? I was traveling between the dark tunnel and here, the dream you're in now. I want to see if I can show you how to do it." Slowly she took the rock out of her pocket.

"Finally," said the boy. "I've been waiting for a millennium. There's this woman who sticks to me like some kind of disease. She'll be upset if I go."

"She'll be all right," said Skey.

The boy's body settled, as if getting ready for a long ride. "So," he said, "how do we get there?"

Everything in Skey paused, hoping. Quietly she said, "I need to hold your hand."

The boy's face leapt in fear. "No way," he said, sliding away from her on the bed. "No touching."

"Why?" asked Skey.

"It'll bring them back," he said. "They'll come back and get me again."

"Who will come back?" she asked. "I thought you forgot everything."

"I don't know who they are," he said. "I just know they come close when someone touches me. Hands. Invisible hands." He shuddered, turning his face left, then right, scanning the darkness behind his closed eyes.

"There are different kinds of touching," said Skey. "There's the dragon's claw."

The boy nodded fiercely.

"And there's me," said Skey. "Just me, holding your hand."

He grimaced, then said hesitantly, "Just my hand?"

"Just your hand," said Skey. "It's the only way I can take you there."

She watched his face struggle between no and yes. How familiar this was to her—being swamped in fear and not knowing why. Fear was so much bigger when you didn't know why.

"It's the way to discover your own story," she said. "All the time you were traveling the dark tunnel, you were looking for something. Searching and searching to understand why."

"Yes," he whispered.

"This will help you find it," she said.

His face twisted, the pain acute. "I can't," he whispered.

"Yes," said Skey, "you can." Carefully she stretched out a hand, the rock in her palm. "My hand is in front of you," she said softly. "You just have to reach out a little."

"Just a little," the boy whispered. She watched his hand tremble, reach forward and pull back. Then, with a small grunt, the boy pushed his hand forward a second time. Swiftly Skey slid her hand under his, and together their hands closed around the rock.

"What's this?" asked the boy in surprise.

"It's a rock," said Skey. "I found it in the tunnel the first time I heard you."

"I thought it was from there," smiled the boy. "I can feel it."

"Now you have to wait a minute," said Skey. "I'm going to go away for a bit, but then I'll come back."

"Just a bit?" asked the boy.

"Just a bit," said Skey. "Promise." She closed her eyes, and the boy and the bedroom disappeared. Instead of a chair, she found herself sitting on cold stone, with a trickle of water running under her leg. In her hand, she still held the rock.

"Lick?" she asked quickly.

"So," he said irritably, his voice inches away. "You decided to show again. What brought you here now? You miss your little carvings?"

"I don't need them anymore," she said.

"Why'd you come back then?" demanded Lick.

"What's the matter?" she asked, pulling back a little.

"It's creepy by myself," snapped Lick. "Too quiet, and I can't see. At least you come and go. I'm stuck here. No one to talk to. It just keeps happening, over and over in my head. I can't get away from it."

"From what?" she asked.

"From those guys coming after me," said Lick. "And my brother. You know—all of it."

"You need to come back," she said.

"Come back where?" Lick asked guardedly.

"Back to your body," she said. "Back to the real world."

"Where it all happened?" hissed Lick. "Even this place is better than that shit."

"Lick," she said urgently, "you're in the wrong place.

Things got mixed up. Reversed. You're supposed to be there, and he's supposed to be here."

"What are you talking about?" demanded Lick.

Taking a deep breath, she launched into it. "You did forget about your brother," she explained carefully. "*Part* of you did. You made a part of yourself forget what your brother did to you, and then you sent that part of you away. He's always lived apart from you, here in the dark tunnel where he could forget, so part of you didn't have to know."

"This is weird," muttered Lick.

"I know it's true," she continued slowly, "because I did the same thing. I got…raped by some guys. That's why I came here, to the dark tunnel, where there could be some peace. Where I could forget. This is where I met the boy in the tunnel, the boy who didn't remember the other part of his life. The boy who told me that names are secrets."

"You told me that," said Lick.

"He told me first," she replied. "The boy in the tunnel told me his name was a secret because he had no name. *You* have the name. I think you and he traded places when those guys from your school beat you up. You came here and pushed him out, and now he's stuck out there, in your body, wandering around. And he doesn't remember anything."

"Lucky him," muttered Lick.

"But he doesn't remember your mother," she said. "He doesn't remember your school. He doesn't even remember his own name."

"So, tell him," yelled Lick.

"He doesn't know what it means," she protested. "Elwin Serkowski doesn't mean anything to him. He's always lived here."

Lick lapsed into silence, his breathing heavy in the dark.

"He's part of you," she said, leaning toward him. "He's the part of you that has peace and quiet in him. *Your* peace and quiet. You need him. He needs you."

"Bullshit," said Lick. In the darkness she could hear his heart thudding deep and slow, pushing everything she had said away away away.

"Listen to me," she said desperately. "Please. Names are not secret, not anymore. Yours is Lick. Mine is Skey."

Beside her, Lick breathed in sharply.

"Why did you wash off your arm, Lick?" Skey asked softly.

"Because...," Lick's voice quivered, and he paused. "Well, because Mom told me what's real is real. You don't need to hold onto the echo."

"I'm real," said Skey, her voice quivering too.

As she spoke, the darkness around them wobbled slightly. She wasn't sure how much longer she could hold onto this place with her mind.

"I remembered what I made myself forget," she said quickly. "The guys who raped me—it was the Dragons. Jigger and Trevor and Balfour and Pedro. All of them. They raped me last May. After it happened, I cut my arms and made myself forget. Then I dreamed myself here to forget even more."

Lick remained silent, breathing in the dark.

"I found you here," Skey continued. "The other part of you, the part of you that had forgotten. But I found you *there* too. At school. Every time I turned around, you were there."

"Yes," Lick whispered.

"I kept...touching you," Skey said. She had started crying. "I needed to touch you, but I didn't know why."

"That was fine with me," said Lick.

"Can I?" she asked quietly. "Can I now? Touch your hand?"

Lick sighed, the sound whispering through the surrounding dark. "Yes," he said.

Reaching forward, she felt his fingertips slide over hers, then brush her palm.

"What's this?" he asked in surprise.

"Just a rock," she said.

Trembling slightly, their hands came together around the rock.

"C'mon, Lick," she said. "Let's go home."

Their hands gripped tighter. For a moment the darkness continued to surround them, and then it dissolved. Briefly, Skey felt herself holding two overlapping hands, Lick's and the boy from the tunnel's, and then the body of Elwin Serkowski appeared opposite her, seated on the bed with his eyes closed. As she watched, his expression took on a look of wonder, as if something new was coming to him, he was breathing different air. Slowly his eyes opened, and she saw that they were alpine green. Lick. The boy from the tunnel. They were both here, together in one face, smiling at her.

Lick let out a quiet string of swear words, and a huge grin split Skey's face. "You can say that again," she said.

They were still holding hands, hers beneath his. Gently she turned their gripped hands upside-down and slid hers away, leaving the rock in his palm. "For you," she said, smiling. "So you can come and go."

Lick and the boy from the tunnel looked at the rock, then at her. "I think," they said in sync, "I don't need it anymore."

With these words, the rock disappeared. One moment, a small gray rock with white markings and rough edges was sitting in Lick's palm, and the next it had returned to the dark tunnel and the meeting place from which it had come.

"Neither do I," said Skey.

Lick shifted slowly on the bed, as if getting used to his body again. "Weird," he muttered. "I feel different. I'm still me, but there's not all those little fidgets running through me all the time."

"You're more relaxed," said Skey.

"Mm," said Lick. "I'll probably never be relaxed, but it's quieter in my head. Darker, sort of like twilight."

"Between the dark and the light," said Skey.

"Uh-huh," said Lick. "And I still remember what happened with my brother, but it's feels over now. Finished. It's not happening to me *right now*, anymore. It's memory, not me."

A smile broke across Skey's face, morning on the ocean. "I like you," she said.

Lick was hit with a sudden massive attack of the fidgets. Then his body quieted. Reaching out, he stroked a finger along the side of Skey's face, and she felt arousal run through her like a soft-breaking wave.

I remember you, smiled the eyes of the boy from the tunnel. *Your stories in the wall.*

Skey took Lick's hand and watched his face burn its usual fierce red as hers flushed in response. There was no dragon's claw here, just shy skin holding shy skin—very, very human. How she wanted this touch, it was true, she felt such joy in it. But at the same time, she knew that touching needed to come slowly for both of them. They would feel their way together gently, she promised herself. It would be like listening to stories told in the dark. Listening carefully. Touching carefully. Listening in love as they touched.

Epilogue

It was the third week of February, and Skey and her mother were packing the last of her things. There wasn't much—the entire job had taken less than ten minutes. All that remained was the small rock that sat on the dresser.

"What's that?" asked her mother, frowning at it.

"Just a rock," said Skey, slipping it into her pocket. "My dreaming rock."

She had picked it up yesterday out of the snow, on her way back from school. It was an ordinary looking rock— gray with white markings and very smooth, nothing her skin could snag and tear on. She had stood in the lockup's parking lot, sliding the rock between her fingers while she observed the wire-crossed windows, and the rock had felt like old pain—a rounded ache, with the sharp edges gone. It was something to remind her of this place.

She hadn't returned to the tunnels since that afternoon, months ago, in Lick's bedroom. Every time she thought of the coming trials, she felt fear, huge waves of it. Sometimes she couldn't breathe, but then she could again. Things went on, she took one step, then another. Then another.

JIGGER, TREVOR, BALFOUR and Pedro were still in the youth detention center. One month from now, she would stand witness at their trials. Her weekly sessions with Larry were helping her to prepare for it, and she would continue to see the social worker even though she had been discharged. Talking to him wasn't that bad, once she had gotten used to the lime chair. Now she sat in it regularly. Her mother no longer attended these sessions. Conversations worked better without her.

One month away. Quickly Skey glanced at the elm outside her window and whispered their pact: *Keep going, keep going.* In response, the tree bowed in ancient grace to her and the wind. She nodded back.

"Your father will be glad to see you," said her mother, moving toward the door.

"Who?" asked Skey carelessly as she closed the small suitcase on her bed.

"Your *father* will be coming over later to welcome you home," said her mother pointedly.

"Let me see," said Skey, counting on her fingers. "June, July, August…it's been nine months. Geez, it's nice of him to make the effort tonight. Actually, I've already asked two of my friends to come over for dinner to help me celebrate."

Her mother stiffened. "And who might they be?" she asked guardedly.

"Don't worry, they don't belong to a gang," Skey assured her. "You remember Lick, the guy Jigger beat up? And I also asked a girl named Tammy Nanji. She's tutoring me at school."

"Well," her mother said huffily, "your father won't be over until later. I suppose it'll be all right. I'll order pizza."

"We just need to make a salad," said Skey. "And dessert.

I asked Tammy to bring the real food. Her mom makes this great stuff."

Her mother sniffed dubiously. "Just make sure they're gone when your father arrives," she said. "This is a special day for him."

As Mrs. Mitchell turned once again to the door, Skey felt a realization open deep within her. She and her mother were different. They looked similar, but biology did not rule. Mrs. Mitchell still stood as she always had, a careful figurine impeccably arranged, waiting for the odd glance her husband might send her way. How much of her mother, Skey wondered, studying the woman before her, was hiding in tunnels of dark and light, crawling away from her own truth? How much had she forgotten?

Pushing up her sleeves, Skey stared at the scars on her forearms. She would always carry them, it was true—she would always be marked. But she knew her own stories now, she knew the truth. With the deepest breath she had ever taken, Skey claimed her future as her own. Never, under any condition, would she become her mother.

"Mom," said Skey, "my friends will come when I need them. They care about me that much. I want you to meet them. I asked Tammy to bring enough food so you could join us."

Her mother gave her another dubious look. "Maybe," she said.

As they came out into the unit, Skey saw Ann hovering nearby. Her sleeves were also pushed up, displaying scars, but in the past three months Ann had gained weight. When she moved now, her bones slid close to the skin, but they weren't as sharp-edged. Ann's flesh was rounding her into old pain.

"I'm still here and you're going," she said forlornly.

"I'll call," said Skey. "Maybe you can come to my house to visit."

Ignoring her mother's sharp gasp, she walked over to the other girl. The hole between their bedroom walls had been fixed months ago, allowing them to continue their nightly wall-tapping game, but they had recently created another version for daylight. Now, as Skey raised her hand, Ann met her with an answering grin. Gently they began tapping on each other's foreheads.

Tap tap, they said with their fingertips. *I'm here too. Lonely on the other side, but I can hear you, tap tap tap. I can hear you, tap tap. I am with you, tap. Lonely, but with you, tap tap. Tap tap tap. With you, tap. Friend.*

WITH A FLOURISH, Terry unlocked the side entrance door and stepped back. Carrying her suitcase through the open doorway, Skey stood in the falling snow and grinned the grin of an escapee.

"Not gonna miss me at all, eh?" Terry grinned back.

"A little," said Skey. "I'll remember you. I'll remember this place."

They stood, Skey outside, Terry inside, the open doorway between them.

"So," said Terry. "Tell me, Skey—what color are you feeling?"

"What color are *you* feeling?" responded Skey.

Terry grimaced. "This means deep thought," she said.

Skey laughed. "I'll call you in a couple of days when you've got it figured out," she said, and turned to follow her mother to the BMW.

But Terry wasn't giving in easily. "Skey," she called, the grin now in her voice. "C'mon, think for me. What color are you feeling?"

The answer came to Skey, wide and sudden as sky. "Blue," she shouted over her shoulder.

"Three o'clock on a summer afternoon?" asked Terry.

Skey turned and began walking backward. "Three o'clock," she said, "and it's really hot, and the radio's playing, and I'm lying in the sun, and I've got nothing to do and I can do anything I want."

She was almost at the car.

"Now you're talking," called Terry.

"I can do anything I want!" shouted Skey. Her entire body was singing. "I can do anything I want!"